TWO MEN.

TORN. TORTURED. *LOVED.*

Though they went their separate ways, Tate Williams and Clay Mortimer have been crazy about each other since their school days. Clay went into the SAS. Tate became a cop. Neither mentioned their attraction to the other. Both sought out danger. Both found it.

Imprisoned and shot in an undercover assignment gone wrong, Tate somehow survived...and found his way back into Clay's arms. His old friend is now the owner of an elite investigation agency and everything any man could want: patient, handsome, commanding. And Clay knows what it takes to survive. But Tate can't bring himself to share all his secrets, nightmares that force him to rebel against *everything*. He finds solace from his past as a graffiti artist, a childhood passion, but his demons drive away all who might care for him. Only when he faces that past—and learns that everyone has tasted despair—can the two men truly be brothers-in-arms...and more.

FEAT OF CLAY

Susan Mac Nicol

A Men of London Romance

www.BOROUGHSPUBLISHINGGROUP.com

FEAT OF CLAY
Copyright © 2015 Susan Elaine Mac Nicol

ISBN 978-1-942886-74-7

This book is dedicated to those out there who battle daily with stress because something in their past haunts them. Sometimes this past cannot easily be put to rest. Depression, bipolar disorder, PTSD and other illnesses affecting mental health are a real challenge for anyone to face.

There is help out there. I encourage those in need to seek it and contact a local organisation or helpline. These are just a few links, but there are many more out there to find out how you can overcome.

http://www.mind.org.uk/information-support/types-of-mental-health-problems/post-traumatic-stress-disorder-ptsd/#.VaYXuJrbLIU

http://www.bipolaruk.org.uk/

http://www.keithmilanomemorialfund.org/

ACKNOWLEDGMENTS

As always I'd like to thank my lovely beta readers Rita R. and JP Bilbao for their valued input with this story. I hope they know how much I appreciate them both.

To the wonderful ladies of Nicky's Starrlettes—Kirsty Vizard, Valerie de George, Janice Birnie, Isa Jones and Joanne Swinney—who do so much to support and encourage me, I thank you from the bottom of my heart. When I'm down or feeling insecure and need a kind word, you ladies are always there to cheer me up and kick my arse to get me back on track. I can't tell you how much I appreciate being told to 'Bloody get out there and just write. We want the next book!'

CONTENTS

FEAT OF CLAY

Chapter 1

Cold. Dark. Silent.

The naked man lying shivering on the cold concrete floor had no idea of the time or day. All he knew was he hurt in every unimaginable place possible. Curled up into a foetal ball, he dug his fingers into cold arms as he tried to hug himself warm. Pain from ragged nails pierced his clammy skin, reminding him he was still alive, albeit in hell. His mouth was so dry from lack of water, he couldn't even cry out anymore. Agony riddled a stomach clenched and knotted from lack of food; he didn't remember the last time he'd eaten.

The only thing keeping him sane was the silence. As long as that remained, he knew he was safe. It was when his captor returned to the room that the air was broken with cries of pain and agonised breaths amidst the whispered gloats from his torturer of just how much his keeper could make him suffer. So when the man on the floor heard the click of the door lock opening, his stomach heaved in fear and pain. He retched strings of bile, knowing that what was coming was far worse than lying broken and beaten half to death on a cold floor.

"Ready for me?" The hated voice was mocking. "Let us begin again."

****

"You bastard, leave me alone. Fucking leave me alone, will you? I won't tell you anything. Fuck off."

Clay Mortimer woke to these words being spat into his ear as an arm beside him thrashed wildly in the throes of a nightmare. It was nothing new; he'd faced this scenario many times. His chest tightened with agonising pain at the utterance of words borne of an experience no man should have endured.

Awake instantly, thanks to his past training in the SAS, Clay reached out and gripped the wrist of the man floundering next to him in their bed. His other hand reached out and pressed itself into his lover's scalp with its thick covering of russet fuzz. Clay's gentle fingers pushed the fevered brow back onto the pillow, trying to stay the man's agitation.

"Tate? Love, it's Clay. Wake up. Come on, wake up. That's it."

As Tate Williams's cloudy hazel eyes opened, panic rife in their depths, Clay stroked his lover's forehead and murmured soothing words of comfort. "Easy, it's just a nightmare. It's over. Look at me." His words grew in urgency as Tate stared at him, no recognition on his face. Clay's stomach tightened and he lost his breath, the familiar anguish with which he lived rising in his chest.

"Look at me, Tate." His voice rose, commanding. "It's Clay. I'm here."

Tate's eyes slowly cleared. "Clay?" He blinked, his gaze focusing as his trembling hand came up and held onto Clay's arm tightly, making him wince. He was used to bruises as Tate came out of his fugues. Clay's partner needed to make sure the man beside him was real, solid.

"I was dreaming…" Tate whispered as he passed his hand across his eyes. "Armerian was there."

Clay swallowed, the mention of the other man's name making his gorge rise, and his blood boil in hate and anger. "Armerian is dead, Tate. He can't hurt you anymore." It was the same litany he repeated every time he drew the man he loved back from the hell he'd been in. Kidnapped, tortured and emotionally abused by a madman just over a year ago, the physical scars on Tate's body may have healed, but his mind was another thing. He was tough and proving steadfast in his attempt to get through each day, but to get his head to its current state had taken a lot of time, tears, frustration and grief. Clay had no doubt there was more of it in store.

Tate nodded slowly and sat up, the covers slipping down his muscled, lightly furred chest, to pool on his hips. "I know. I remember." His upper body was soaked in sweat, the dark curls on his torso damp and matted. Faint silver scars transacted his belly and ribs like a grid. Two deeper, rounder and thicker indents marked his upper left shoulder and pectoral muscle. Another one splayed across the left side of his ribs.

Clay sighed. He rose naked from their bed and walked over to the chair. A damp towel still sat there from their recent shower-sex marathon. He picked it up, went back to Tate, sat down beside him and dabbed the soft fabric across his face then across the pools of moisture on his body. Tate watched him do it, and Clay was glad to see his lips curve in a small smile.

"You're always looking after me. My very own defender—my knight in shining armour."

Clay snorted loudly. "Well, aren't we being literary. I just like to make sure you're okay, that's all." He finished what he was doing and threw the towel to the floor. He stood up to move around to his side of the bed and Tate reached out with both hands to grip Clay's hips.

Despite the fact his partner had just woken from a nightmare, Clay's cock stirred at the feel of Tate's warm hand on his skin and the desire in his eyes. Sex had become something of a sleeping aid to Tate, as he used it to dispel the nightmares he held. For the most part, Clay was fine with that. Sometimes, though, he felt as if he was simply a distraction, a living, breathing placebo for Tate to find his inner solace. He supposed wryly that there were worse ways for his partner to deal with his issues than using Clay as a human dildo.

"Stay there," Tate murmured as Clay's dick began its slow rise upward. "I want to taste you. Then you can fuck me."

As Tate's lips closed over his cock, Clay closed his eyes and gave in to the pleasure.

****

After Tate was sated and once more resting uneasily, Clay lay watching the restless form of his lover. The covers had fallen off and Tate lay on his side, back to Clay. Tate's honey-toned skin and the firm curve of his backside were a welcome sight. Clay reached out gently and traced the tattoo on Tate's right arse cheek. It was a dragon, teeth bared, wings spread, in shades of grey and black. It covered the whole taut muscle and while it looked stunning, Clay knew it hid something much more sinister.

Beneath the powerful beast roaring on Tate's flesh lay the word *Reino,* carved out with a scalpel in Tate's skin by the man who sixteen months ago had kept Clay's lover prisoner for four days, tortured him, then shot him three times and left him for dead in a city street. A snarling twist of deception had left Tate the victim after his undercover drug sting went bad. The dragon covered up what Tate thought was a shameful scar, but Clay, who'd chosen the image for him, had always thought it reflected his lover's inner strength and resilience.

Tate stirred and murmured sleepily and Clay hastily moved his fingers away so he didn't wake Tate completely. He settled back in the bed and pulled the duvet up over them both.

I hope he manages to sleep, was Clay's last conscious thought as he sank into darkness. *I don't know how long he can go on like this.*

Chapter 2

Tate sighed heavily as he fielded his way through the three computer screens set up in his home office. As a researcher and strategist for Clay's business, Mortimer Investigations, Tate spent a lot of time checking out information, inspecting facts and fiction supplied by snitches and leads and finding the real truth behind the stories. He'd always been a geek, loving gadgets and anything digital.

"I suppose it's just as well I had this kind of interest now that I'm 'retired' out of field work," he muttered to himself as he logged into yet another government agency site to collate information for his boss and partner. "I'd rather be out shooting someone though."

That thought made him scowl. He'd been trying to convince Clay he could go back to field work as one of his investigators, but Clay was adamant; Tate wasn't ready for that yet. Clay had a rod of steel when it came to his business, putting personal feelings aside, doing what was best for his company and his other operatives. He felt Tate would compromise the others' safety. No amount of cajoling or seduction techniques would work. Tate had tried them all.

He yawned and stood up to stretch his legs. His side ached where the second bullet had cut through like butter, the right arse cheek with its sensitive scar always appreciating an opportunity not to be sat on. Tate caught sight of his reflection in the mirrored glass of the sliding door leading out to the garden. He assessed himself critically.

He saw a clean shaven, well-built man of thirty-three, his body toned and muscled, with buzz-cut hair and hazel eyes. There were dark bags under his eyes and he reached up and touched them with a frown. His old but comfortable tee shirt rode up as he lifted his arms to stretch, and he got a sense of satisfaction as seeing his stomach was still tight, thanks to the regime of crunches and sit-ups he did every day in his well-kitted out home gym in the spare room. A dark treasure trail led down to his groin, to the waistband of his joggers, which sat low on his hips.

Tate grinned as he remembered this morning—Clay tracing that trail with his mouth, those warm, tantalising lips teasing and sucking until reaching Tate's needy dick. He loved Clay's mouth, the one that could look so stern and forbidding sometimes then melted into an expression of love and desire at seeing Tate. He also loved the fact that Clay could suck cock with those lips like no one else could.

He took a deep breath as the pleasurable memory gave way to one not so pleasant. Yet another nightmare last night had taken a lot out of him. They *had* been getting better though, going from virtually every night to two or three times a week. They left him debilitated and on edge. Since the shooting it had been rough for them both, no matter how much work-designated therapy Tate attended.

He scowled at his reflection. "Still no matter how much 'meditation' I do before bed, I'm still a fucking wimp, waking up and having to have my man wiping my damn face like I'm a kid. I was an undercover drug cop, for Christ's sake. I should have more discipline and self-control." He knew, deep down, the feelings of guilt, shame and self-recrimination lurking deep in his soul had as much to do with the nightmares as what had been done to him.

He kicked out moodily at a wastepaper basket sitting innocently at the side of his desk. It fell, rolled over and dispersed copious amounts of wadded-up paper onto the carpet. Tate's temper flared, something that happened all too often, and his foot lunged out, scattering the paper to the four corners of the room.

"Fuck you," he growled as he stomped and beat one unfortunate ball of paper into a flattened mess. "Damn you all to fucking hell." He didn't really know who he was swearing at, but the violent action felt good. When he finally stopped, his breathing faster and a slight ringing in his ears from the pressure in his head, there was a loud clapping noise from the door.

Adrenaline rushing through his veins, he swung around to see the tall, wide shouldered figure of his lover behind him.

"Tate Williams: one, Paper Ball: nil." Clay stepped into the room. "Do you feel better now? If you needed to release any energy, we could always have sparred for a while in the gym." He flashed a quick smile. "Or we could have done something else just as energetic and far more…pleasurable."

Tate waved a hand at him, fear rising in his throat. "It just shows you how bloody useless I am. I didn't even hear you come in. What if you had been someone else?"

Clay's eyes darkened. "I have keys, remember? For all three locks on the front door. No one's getting into Fort Tate, love."

It was their joke. After he'd been tortured by a maniac, Tate had equipped his flat in Kentish Town with alarms, sensors, extra steel locks and other paraphernalia to make sure that in Fort Tate, as Clay had coined it, Tate felt safe. It was probably not needed—after all, the man who'd hurt him was dead—but his paranoia ran deep. There had been a time when he'd left his doors open and hadn't had panic buttons on the wall. To be fair, a lot of the protective measures had been Clay's urging. The man had been a wreck after seeing Tate in the hospital, and Tate's safety and protection had become Clay's number-one priority. Sometimes it felt like a warm blanket; other times it felt like suffocating smog. As no one knew the extent of their relationship as lovers, the two men still kept separate homes. Clay had a huge Victorian house in Twickenham, which Tate loved unreservedly, while Tate had his ground-floor flat. It was an ongoing thorn in Tate's side, keeping their secret.

Clay wasn't convinced it was the right thing to be open about them yet. "Tate, the job I do involves making enemies," he'd said quietly one night after a bout of passion. "If they know we're together in this way, it gives them an edge. They can use you to get to me, hurt you again. And I will never let that happen. You need more time to get over what happened to you. Let's wait a bit longer."

Tate didn't really appreciate being treated as if he were made of glass. In any case, he thought anyone watching them would probably make an assumption anyway about their relationship, but he hadn't been able to budge Clay on his decision. The man was as stubborn as hell.

Tate snorted as he moved over to kiss his partner. "Yeah, well, still."

He reached up to frame Clay's stubbled cheeks with his hands as his lover brought his face down to kiss him. Large hands came out and spanned Tate's waist, drawing him closer. Clay smelt of Fahrenheit, and shampoo and man. He was strong, muscled and wiry, and taller than Tate at six foot four.

Tate liked slotting into Clay's arm like a piece of a well-fitting jigsaw. One lock of jet-black hair swept over Clay's forehead and he raised a hand to absently brush it away. Long, dark eyelashes—like a giraffe's, Tate always thought—framed piercing green eyes that currently gazed at him with affection. Tate's man was indeed damned handsome and Tate never tired of looking at him.

Tate nudged Clay's hip. "What are you doing here anyway? I thought you had some fancy schmancy meeting with Draven?"

Clay shrugged. "I did. We got through the briefing quicker than I'd expected. He's on his way to Spain tomorrow night for a couple of days on the Medina Pharmaceutical case you did the research for. He'll get that sorted in no time, no doubt. So I thought I'd surprise you." He grinned. "I didn't think I'd find you kickboxing with a piece of paper when I got here."

Tate nodded. "He's going to track down Rupert Medina then?" He might not be in the field but Clay was always willing to talk about his cases with Tate and kept him in the loop.

Medina was the owner of a profitable and well-known pharmaceutical company that'd been selling illegal and ineffective versions of drugs for various life-threatening illnesses. From his involvement in the case, Tate knew at least ten patients had died using the company's ineffective and low-quality products. It had become a nationwide hunt to bring the man to justice and Clay had happened to find him first. Things had gotten nasty; one law enforcement officer had already died in trying to bring Medina to justice and Tate hoped both Clay and Draven would be careful.

Clay's face darkened, his face grim. "Medina looks as if he's fled to Spain, hence Draven going over there to find him and bring him back. That murderer is fucking lucky it's not me. I'd have no hesitation shooting the bastard and leaving him in the bay for the fishes to feed on."

Tate had no doubt of that. One of the things that turned him on about Clay was his tough, no-holds-barred attitude in his work. Seeing Clay in full macho and interrogator mode got Tate harder than he'd ever thought possible.

"And the toxic waste case?" Tate enquired. "What's the latest on that one?"

Clay's eyes narrowed and his nostrils flared. "We think we've found a connection to someone who might know what's going on. We're trying to find him so I can ask him some questions." He smiled wolfishly. "The man won't know what's fucking hit him when I finally get hold of him." His emerald eyes glinted in devilish anticipation. It was damned sexy and Tate had no doubt the unfortunate individual would experience the indomitable force of Clay. It was as sexy as hell.

"How are Draven and Taylor's wedding plans coming along?" Tate asked as he traced the five o'clock shadow on Clay's face, charcoal black laced with silver, like his thick head of hair. Clay had only just turned thirty-six but Tate was forever teasing him about those errant silver strands.

Clay chuckled. "Still on the go. Both of them are in no hurry; they're fine with a long engagement, and it's only been six months. Neither of them wants a big wedding. Knowing them both, we'll probably just get an invite one day to something low-key but intimate." He snorted with laughter. "Probably up in the wilds of Scotland or something. Taylor apparently has this thing for the Highlands. I think it's more he enjoys the men in kilts myself." Tate's nodded. "Wow, that's...cool." He flicked a guilty glance at his partner as he moved away from Clay's embrace.

Clay's face was noncommittal but no doubt he was remembering, as was Tate, the night nearly eight months ago when he had asked Tate whether marriage, even kids, might be on the cards for them at a future date. Tate had been surprised, given Clay's stance on not making their relationship public. Clay had said quietly had said that he liked to think there would be a time when they could shout it from the rooftops.

Tate had said no to marriage and kids. He'd been rather more aggressive than he'd meant to be in his refusal. He'd still been so fucked up at the time, and hadn't felt he could make that kind of decision then. He'd gotten over it, as had Clay—the man had a knack for putting things behind him and moving on—but Tate knew he'd hurt his lover. And he hated himself for it.

"Don't worry," Clay said softly. "I'm not going to mention it again." He smiled but Tate saw the wariness behind it.

His stomach lurched and his heart ached at the look in Clay's expressive jade-green eyes. "I didn't think that. Stop putting words in my mouth. And we both know I wasn't ready for that conversation yet."

Clay regarded him evenly. "I get it; don't worry. Like I said, I won't bring it up again."

Tate swallowed. He'd known Clay since he was six years old, and Clay had been nine. They'd grown up together in Guildford in Surrey, gone to the same schools, albeit Clay ahead of him. They'd discovered they liked guys together and bonded as unlikely best friends.

Tate decided to let it go. "Lucy called. She said Rick got that promotion he wanted. I'm pretty proud of him." Lucy was Tate's older sister. Rick was his nephew and following in his uncle's footsteps in the police force. He was the only other person who knew the true nature of Clay and Tate's relationship. There'd been an unfortunate incident at Tate's home once when Rick had popped around and found them in flagrante delicto. It had been a few months after the shooting and they'd both been careless. Rick had muttered darkly that he needed to bleach his eyes now he'd seen Clay buried balls deep in his uncle.

Clay smiled warmly. He had a soft spot for Rick. "He did? That's great news. He's a great policeman; he deserves it."

Tate nodded. "Lucy's lucky to have such a level-headed kid. He'll go far."

The note of longing he heard in his voice for his old job didn't appear to escape Clay, as his lover's face darkened. The man knew him too well, knew that Rick had something Tate could no longer have. His career as an undercover cop was over, as his cover had been blown, and no amount of persuasion could make the powers that be reinstate him. When Clay had offered him the research position, Tate had decided it would fill in until he could get back into the saddle one hundred percent.

Tate found himself pulled into a fierce kiss, one that made him forget for a while, as Clay's mouth bruised his in an act of possession. Clay's mouth tasted of sweet sauce and burger, mixed with the sweet taint of Coke. When they finally drew apart, Tate still breathless, he wiped a finger across Clay's shining lips.

"You've been eating those damn Big Mac things again. How the hell do you not put on a stone and look like a house? Do you know what that garbage is doing to your cholesterol levels?" Tate tended to eat a lot healthier than his lover. He was quite a fan of salads, lean meats and low-fat foods.

Clay chuckled. "Like I tell Draven, tequila, hot sex and the gym keeps that weight away." He patted his toned stomach. "The hot sex part being my favourite bit of that."

Tate's dick plumped up in his jeans, happy with that scenario too. He pulled Clay's mouth down for another heated kiss. Maybe he could persuade Clay to get his clothes off and fuck him.

Judging from Clay's groan of satisfaction and the hardness pressed against Tate's stomach as Tate explored his mouth with his tongue, Clay would need little persuasion.

They were interrupted when Clay's mobile rang.

He unglued his lips from Tate's and scowled fiercely as he reached into his trouser pocket to answer it. "This had better be an emergency or someone's arse is getting kicked. I said no fucking calls." His eyes smouldered. "I had plans for you this afternoon."

Tate's insides danced with pleasure at the promise of those words. Clay winked then turned and Tate watched as he went outside onto the small balcony overlooking the green.

He bent down and picked up the crumpled piece of paper lying under the desk, dropping it into the waste bin. As he did, a series of loud, stuttering bangs from outside rent the air, rapid fire sounds that caused Tate to freeze. His heartbeat sped up, his throat dried out and he reached out to grab the edge of his desk as dizziness assailed him. Flickers of light blurred his vision as the noises outside rose in crescendo and the shrill sound of a siren could be heard in the distance. Flashes of memory sped through his mind like the fast forwarding of a DVD film. Immersed in the roar in his ears, he heard the faint echoes of his own voice crying out as bullets smacked into his body. Remembered pain and humiliation soaked Tate like a drenching acid rain from hell, burning and scalding him with his own shame and guilt.

"Bloody kids; they shouldn't be allowed to sell firecrackers until Guy Fawkes—Tate, are you okay?" Clay's worry and concern settled over Tate like a stifling fire blanket, dulling his senses, causing his limbs to become heavy as he struggled to get his racing heart under control. Vomit welled in his throat, rancid, foul-tasting bile that reached his mouth, causing him to gag and retch onto the floor. Clay's hand steadied his arm and Tate lashed out in anger and self-hatred as he pushed him away.

"Leave me alone, Clay," he snarled as he wiped his mouth. The darkness in his soul claimed him; sneering caustic jibes about just how pathetic he was buzzed in his ears. "I'm not a child and I don't need you picking up the pieces every time I have a meltdown."

The words were meant to hurt and yet for the life of him, he regretted hurling them at the man he loved. A chance children's prank and yet another realisation of his frailty had ignited a self-hating flame that couldn't be extinguished.

"I wasn't 'picking up the pieces'," Clay said evenly. "You were having a panic attack. I wanted to make sure…"

"You wanted to make sure that I was all right, that the sound of fucking bangs hadn't driven me crazy and that poor, damaged Tate could still function." Tate spat the words and Clay's eyes darkened as his lips thinned. "Well, you know what? You're fighting a losing battle. Because Tate *isn't* okay. He's a useless piece of shit who'll always be like this, so you'd be better off moving on and finding someone who can cope with hearing kids letting off firecrackers in the middle of the fucking street and who doesn't wake you up in the middle of the night with fucking bad dreams."

Tate was on a roll and he had no way to stop himself. That was how it worked. The freight train that was his tormented psyche gained momentum and rolled forward, crushing everything in its path.

"Christ, I love you, Clay, you know that, but I can't take this anymore. I need some space. I need to be alone and figure this out."

Clay moved forward, the bulk of his body both commanding and familiar. Tate wanted to enfold himself in those arms, feel the beat of Clay's strong heart against his chest, the warmth of his man's body against his, but he couldn't let that happen. He needed to get his head right, be someone Clay could respect again, not this broken, haunted man in front of him—a weakling.

"We tried that," Clay said softly, the pain in his eyes stabbing into Tate's heart with every blink of his eyelashes. "Remember? I came and fetched you and brought you home."

Tate stared at him. "You broke into the hotel I was staying at, tied me up and brought me back to that safe house, where you continued to lock me up while you talked the shit out of me. Some people call that kidnapping."

Clay took a shuddering breath. "I call it love. And it worked, didn't it? Those slashes on your wrist healed and you told me you wouldn't do it again. You even started going to therapy again."

Instinctively, Tate stared down at the scars on his wrists, reminders of that time ten months ago when he'd decided he'd had enough. He'd booked a cheap room in a hotel, drank himself stupid then attempted to slash his wrists. He was a cop; he knew how to do it properly, and yet he'd slashed across instead of down. Something had held him back. He had no doubt had he done it the right way, he'd be dead now.

Clay had tracked him down. How, he never knew, but his lover had his ways. He'd been forcibly bundled him into a van and a doctor had come to the house to patch him up. Then Clay had kept him under luxurious house arrest for a week in a radical one-man intervention. Tate had sworn at him, cursed him, but in his heart of hearts he'd been glad Clay hadn't let him die that night. His suicidal tendencies had abated over these long months and he was trying to put that whole sorry episode in the past.

"Yeah, well, maybe if we'd had someone else to talk to, had friends around that we could share stuff with, it would have been better for us both. Instead we creep around like a dirty secret because you're scared for me." He slammed his fist down on the table. "God knows I've tried to get you to make our relationship public but you insist on molly coddling me, hiding me for my *own good*. It's been over a year that we've been living like this, Clay." He spat the words then paused, his chest heaving.

Clay folded his arms across his broad chest and observed with tired and shadowed eyes. This conversation was familiar to both of them.

"You know why I feel that's the right thing to do, Tate. We've discussed it."

"That doesn't mean I've agreed." Tate passed a hand over tired, sore eyes. "Look, I need to be alone for a bit. I think you should go, and I'll call you when I'm ready. Leave your house keys."

Clay's eyes filled with pain so deep Tate wanted to vomit again. "Tate, love, please don't do this. Don't push me away."

Tate swallowed bile. "Go, Clay. Like I said, I don't want you around right now. I need to get my head round all this again."

His lover shook his head. "No."

He stood firm and Tate knew he had to do something to get Clay to go, so he could wallow in his own self-pity and come to grips with the disease that was his damaged self. Maybe that way he could become more of the man Clay needed.

"I *will* fucking hit you," he warned as he strode toward his partner and held out his hands for the keys. "Make no mistake. Give me the keys."

Clay's hands clenched but he made no move. "No."

"I swear I'll take them from you." Tate became desperate. The darkness inside him swelled to a crescendo and sent grasping, greedy ice-cold feelers out to clasp his twisted guts.

"Then try." There was steel in Clay's expression, a *don't fuck with me* attitude that Tate had seen fell bigger and stronger men than him. But he had one thing on his side. Clay *loved* him. And sometimes love was blind.

Tate made as if to lower his arm, and knowing Clay as well as he did, seeing the imperceptible lowering of his defences for someone he loved, he struck at a time when the man wasn't expecting it. His fist shot out, catching Clay on his jaw. Clay gave a shout of pain and surprise as he stumbled back, hands instinctively coming up to block himself. Tate moved in for another strike and was stopped by the look of despair that crossed Clay's face.

Clay held up his hands in surrender. "I'm not going to fight you, baby," he whispered, his face bleak. "I get it. I'll go." His hands trembled as he reached down and took the house keys from his pocket and threw them on the floor. "There. Satisfied? You got what you wanted."

No I didn't. I only got what I need. What you *need right now.*

The sour taste in Tate's mouth intensified. "Thank you."

Clay nodded curtly, but his eyes were haunted. "Just promise me you aren't going to do anything stupid, Tate. That's all I'm asking. And keep seeing Doctor Jakes for your therapy." His voice shook. "I'm sorry you think I'm so possessive. I want to let go, I promise, it's just that…" he shrugged helplessly. "I don't want you getting hurt again."

"I'm not going to try and off myself, Clay," Tate said quietly. "I promise. I just need some time. A few days, maybe a week. Then I'll call you."

"I'll be waiting." Clay made as if to touch Tate then reconsidered and dropped his hand. "Call me soon. Remember I love you. Never doubt that. Never forget it."

Clay turned and left without a backward glance, leaving Tate standing there, sick to his stomach and cursing a dead sadist with all the vitriol in his soul. He stared at the closed door for a few minutes, trapped in his memories and filled with self-loathing.

Why the fuck did I just chase away the best thing that ever happened to me?

Deep down inside Tate knew why, but it was a secret only he and his therapist shared. And *that* had only come about because Dr. Natalie Jakes was a master at getting to a person's core—of digging deep and finding the vulnerabilities inside. Tate knew he was lucky to have her; he also knew he *needed* her. Needed her help in coming to grips with what had happened to him and what he'd done, but that didn't make it any easier in the telling of his tale. His shameful secret was something he regretted every day and not yet something he was prepared to tell Clay about. God knew how Clay would react.

The operation with Sonny Armerian had taken more from Tate than his dignity and self-confidence; it had taken his soul.

Tate turned and slumped down on the couch, covering his eyes with trembling hands.

"I'm going to have to tell him soon," he whispered to himself. "This can't go on like this, making us both miserable. I just need the right time to do it…"

He lay back on the couch and huddled into a ball, hugging himself tight. The devil on his shoulder gloated that if he did, he could lose the man he loved. The angel on the other told him softly that Clay loved him regardless and Tate should take the chance.

I guess I'll have to decide which camp I'm in. Heaven or hell.

Tate closed his eyes and let the darkness of sleep claim him.

Chapter 3

Clay peered blearily at his watch, trying to see the time through blurred eyes. He tried to focus on the swimming digits and raised his wrist closer to his eyes. Around him, the chatter and noise of the bar buzzed in his ears.

"It's nearly midnight, boss. Time to be heading home, I think," the amused voice of Draven Samuels murmured into Clay's left ear.

Clay grinned at him. "Dray, how the hell are you?" He squinted at his employee and friend. "What are you doing here? Is Taylor with you? How did you find me?"

Draven shook his head with a grin as he sat down on the barstool next to Clay. He waved at the bartender.

"Can I have some strong black coffee for this man, please? Just keep them coming."

The bartender nodded and turned to the back of the bar to prepare the drinks.

Draven's dark eyes regarded Clay with some curiosity. "No, Taylor is home in bed. The same place you need to be I think. And you always come here when you're upset. This is your go-to place." He narrowed his eyes. "You, my friend, are as pissed as a newt. Considering you don't normally drink like this, I'm thinking Taylor's sixth sense was right. Something is wrong."

"Taylor had a premoniti—" Clay's voice faltered. "A vision of me?" Taylor Abelard was a psychic—a damned good one that Clay and his police colleagues sometimes used for a case. He was also Draven's fiancé.

Clay's stomach roiled and he swallowed bile. He'd had this acidic taste in his mouth ever since Tate had kicked him out of his apartment.

"He woke me up in a panic saying something was wrong with you." Draven's tone was dry. "And we all know I don't ignore my man when he has one of his touchy-feely things going on." He reached over and touched Clay's chin gently. "From the looks of it, he was right. Who hit you?"

The fierce protectiveness in Draven's voice gave Clay a warm, mushy feeling. Draven was right; Clay didn't often drink to excess and certainly not here on his own, in his favourite bar. Being told to leave and seeing the pain in Tate's eyes when he'd left had made forgetting the image through alcohol a more palatable option. His head swam and he passed a trembling hand over his eyes, trying to clear them.

"Tate hit me. He was scared. I didn't want to fight him though. So I left."

"Who's Tate, Clay? The man you've been seeing?" Clay had never made his relationship with Tate public at work, not even to Draven. He had his reasons. Draven knew though that he had someone special. Maybe now was the time to share the news with a man he respected and liked more than anyone else in his life—other than Tate.

Clay snorted. "Yep, my secret lover, the man I've wanted for what seems like forever. He kicked me out of his home tonight."

He heard the anguish in his own voice and swallowed. The bartender placed a steaming cup of coffee down in front of him and he stared at it as his eyes prickled.

"Drink the coffee, boss man," Draven muttered quietly. "Then I'll take you home."

Clay picked up the cup and took a large gulp from it. The liquid burnt his lips and he swore. "Fuck. That hurt."

Draven's lips curved in a small smile. "You *are* in a state. So why did Tate kick you out… or hit you?" The swift change of subject was a Draven special, designed to put people off guard and take them unawares. Clay should know; he'd taught him his interrogation techniques. As a senior operative of Mortimer Investigations, and probably the best, Draven was a man not to underestimate. Clay really needed to share and he could think of no better man to trust.

Clay shrugged. "He needed time on his own. He's fucked up. I've tried to hold it together but tonight…" his voice trailed off. "Tonight he really flipped out again. He has panic attacks after the shooting incident. He gets aggressive. He thinks he's weak, but he's not. He's the strongest man I know."

Draven's eyes widened. "Your friend Tate—is this Tate Williams that we're talking about? Taylor's friend Rick's uncle?"

Tate's shooting had made the papers, so it was public knowledge.

Clay waggled a finger at him. He was feeling sicker by the minute and the black coffee wasn't really helping. "Now you know my secret. I shouldn't have told you; it might put Tate in danger. You can't tell anyone else. Except maybe Taylor, 'cos I know he won't talk. But God, Draven, I'm so tired. He didn't deserve what happened to him and I can't make it right for him." His heart ached and he wanted nothing more than to go home to Tate's house, gather his man in his arms and kiss the shit out of him.

Draven's watchful eyes regarded him. "He got shot, Clay. That's bound to fuck anyone up."

Clay snorted sadly. "That's not all that happened to him, Dray. Armerian got his hands on him long before the shooting. Did things to him that you can't imagine, including some stuff Tate's never told me about but I suspect it was worse than he's told me." His suspicion that Tate had suffered more than physical torture—that he'd suffered some form of sexual abuse at Sonny Armerian's hand—lived deep in his gut and made him crazy with hate for a man who was already dead.

Draven stiffened. "Tate was *tortured* by Sonny Armerian? *That* never made the papers." Of course it made sense that Draven would know exactly who he meant when he said the name 'Armerian.' The man was an astute investigator and thrived on all things law enforcement.

Clay waved a hand. His own hand movements made him dizzy. "No, it was all hushed up. That motherfucker held him for four days, trying to get him to spill the beans about the whole drug sting operation. The bastard did unspeakable things to him, and he shot him. *Three fucking times.* Armerian thought he was dead so he pushed him out of a moving car in front of the gym where they'd met. Thank God Tate is made of tough stuff." He finished his coffee and like magic another one appeared.

His friend let out a long sigh. "I always knew there was more to that story than was made public. Tate was working undercover in the drug squad then?"

Clay nodded. "Yes. He'd been in deep cover for close to three months. They were trying to find the head honcho that Armerian reported into, someone really high up in the organisation…" He closed his eyes, remembering the drawn features and pale face of his lover. "I don't even know the full story about his time undercover; he never talks about it. But Tate was a mess, living on a knife edge."

It had been a difficult time for them both, in their then-relationship as "just friends." Staying apart and only making contact with each other when the need arose. They'd had to be ultra-careful, but both men were trained in techniques to keep themselves safe and stay off the grid.

"Armerian was killed by a car bomb about two weeks after Tate was shot," Draven observed, his eyes searching Clay's. "Was that your doing?"

There was no accusation in Draven's tone, simply curiosity. Men like him knew the value of revenge.

Clay shook his head tiredly. "I went looking for him while Tate was in protective custody at the hospital. I was going to kill that bastard for what he did to him. But the Renaldo cartel got to him first. He pissed them off and they took him out." He sipped his coffee. "I was following Armerian. I watched as he got into his Maserati and the thing blew sky high. That's how I knew he was finally dead. It was such a fucking relief. At least I knew they wouldn't come back to finish Tate off. The other cartel members all defected to Renaldo and thankfully they didn't care about a half-dead man."

"And you never trusted me to tell me all this? You dealt with this on your own?" Draven's voice was pained. "I thought we were friends, Clay. You know I'd keep any secrets you shared with me. You did the same for me with Jude." Clay remembered the heartache when Jude, Draven's little brother who was injured in a car accident and left comatose, was at the point of never getting better. Draven had made an agonising decision to turn off his life support, something which haunted him to this day.

Clay reached out and gripped Draven's muscled arm tightly. "I couldn't. Tate was so bloody damaged and I couldn't risk anything else happening to him. You and I have enemies, Draven. It's the nature of the work we do. Tate has always been my Achilles' heel. No matter what our relationship, I couldn't have anyone finding out how much he means to me and using him against me. If they'd known exactly what he was to me, it would have made it worse."

Draven stared at him and then nodded slightly. "That makes sense. People could get to you through me then to Tate. I'd do the same if it was Taylor who'd been hurt like that."

Clay's head was clearing a little now. "I know I'm a bit paranoid, and Tate's told me the same thing. It's just hard, you know?" He stared down. "I've known him since we were kids. We lived on the same street; our parents were friends." He got lost in the half-full coffee cup. God it felt good telling someone about this.

"He was three years younger than me. We went through school together, came out together and we were best friends. But I'd always known he was more than that to me, even when we were so young." He drew a deep breath. "I needed to stop any temptation before I did something illegal to Tate, so I went straight into the RAF at eighteen. Tate was only fifteen then. He stayed behind to finish secondary school and then college. I was travelling around so much, never in one place, and it was tough to see each other, apart from an occasional meet-up when both of us were in town together. We kept in touch with Skype, messages, emails…God, the emails. I think I must have a damn novel on my computer."

His voice trailed off. "Tate found his way into the police force and worked his way up to detective in the drug squad. I'd joined the SAS and was never around." He snorted softly. "Six years ago we each found time to meet up face to face again at a family function. It was like physically being apart had never happened. We took up as mates again but I definitely wanted more. Tate'd had a couple of old relationships and wasn't ready to start anything with anyone, least of all me. I just didn't think he thought of me that way."

Draven shifted on the barstool and shot a glance at the bartender, who was obviously waiting for them to leave so he could close up. Draven ignored him. "So you became close again?"

Clay nodded. "Yes. Then all the shit happened. Somehow Armerian found out about him. We still don't know how. The investigation is ongoing, but it's unlikely we'll ever see any further developments." He stared unseeingly at the bar counter. "From the time Tate woke up in hospital, I was there for him. Things changed between us after that. I guess a near-death experience makes you reconsider your priorities." He grinned wryly. "A couple of months after his shooting, we had sex for the first time. It blew my mind. What was equally mind-blowing was when he confessed he'd always had a thing for me but had never acted on it. He didn't think I felt the same way about him and neither of us wanted to blow the friendship we'd had since childhood."

"No. Just blow each other maybe," Draven observed drily. "Christ, you two were stubborn arseholes not admitting your feelings for one another." He snorted. "I can relate to that." He scowled. "I always knew you had someone special, friend or lover. You were always so damn secretive about the man in your life."

Clay nodded and then wished he hadn't as his head exploded. "I've always loved him; I just didn't tell him. It was fucking torture."

The bartender cleared his throat. "Gents, I need to close up the bar. Sorry about that but…" he rolled his eyes. "It's way past closing time."

Draven stood up. "Come on. Let's make sure you get into a taxi home. The tube won't be running now."

Clay drained the dregs from his coffee cup and got to his feet. He stumbled and Draven's strong arm gripped his elbow.

"Easy, champ. Good thing I'm here." The two men made their way outside and Clay's head swam as the cold air hit him. The empty feeling in his chest amplified at the fact that he was going home to his empty house. True, he and Tate had their own places, but more often than not, when he got home, Tate would be found curled up on Clay's old, comfortable sofa, in sweats and a cut-off tee shirt. The bad days were something they faced together; the good days were heaven. Only now Tate had decided his past was his cross alone to bear.

"I don't want to lose him, Dray," Clay muttered as Draven opened the taxi door and motioned him in, giving the driver his address.

"I know," his friend said softly. "But you've had your drink binge and gotten it out of your system; now work on getting him back. You're Clay Mortimer, for God's sake. You can figure this out. Just keep being there for him and give him the space he needs." His eyes darkened. "One word of advice. Tate is a grown man, Clay. You have to let go sometime, let him be his own man, take his own risks. Or you're going to stifle him. Especially given what he was. The man's used to taking care of himself, taking risks."

Clay blinked at him. "Since when you did you get to be so damn wise?" he murmured. "Is that Taylor's doing? That man has been good for you, you know that?"

"I'm very lucky to have him," Draven agreed. "And you'll get your man back too. Just go home, sleep it off and I'll see you tomorrow. You know where I am if you need me. Make sure you call me if you do. Don't be fucking Captain Lonerguy and try and do it on your own."

He stepped back onto the pavement and rapped his knuckles on the roof of the taxi. As it pulled away, Clay leaned back into the vinyl-smelling seat and closed his eyes. Draven's words about letting Tate go echoed in his ears. They stayed with him long after he finally got home and stumbled into bed for a restless, uneasy sleep.

Chapter 4

Watching a film containing multiple car chases and picking up all
the continuity errors in the story wasn't really the way Tate wanted
to spend his evening, but after a day of nonstop web browsing and
compiling reports for work, he needed something mindless to
distract himself.

He lolled on his two-seater couch, clad in old joggers and a soft
sweatshirt, a bowl of Kung Pao chicken on his chest as he watched
one of the *Fast and Furious* movies. He picked at his food as he
watched Vin Diesel getting it on with some busty blonde. Not that *he*
wouldn't have minded getting it on with Vin, of course. He'd bet on
the fact that if Vin was gay, he'd be one hell of a power bottom.
Everybody else thought he'd be a top but Tate thought differently.
Tate rather fancied that idea of having a naked, buff Vin Diesel bent
down on the bed, muscular, delectable arse in the air.

Thinking of sexy arses made him think of Clay. It had been four
days since he'd last seen him. Clay had texted and Tate had replied,
and the conversation had been fairly non- committal. Clay asked
how he was and Tate told him he was fine. Both of them knew he
was lying. Tate's soul burned with the shame of pushing Clay away.
He ached with his need for the man who'd turned his world upside
down and he languished in despair once again at how he managed to
keep fucking up anything good that they had.

Tate had been to his usual session at his therapist. She'd
subjected him to some gruelling interrogation and once again given
him a lot of perceptive insights. He always felt better after seeing her.
Dr Natalie Jakes was a master manipulator and an excellent
psychologist, plus she didn't take Tate's bullshit. She'd been really
miffed to hear he'd kicked Clay out. Her small, elfin face had
creased in a scowl behind her spectacles and she'd chastised him in
that gentle, completely *I'm going to kick your arse* way she had.

"I appreciate you feeling that way, Tate," she'd said gently.
"But Clay is the one person who can help you in this struggle you
have. Take your time off, but don't take too long. Don't fuck it up
for yourself. I know you're frustrated because he protects you too
much and that *does* need to change for both of you to be comfortable.

He can't wrap you in cotton wool too much longer. But give him a little more time."

Her words had struck fear into Tate's heart that Clay may get tired and give up on him, or that they'd be forever hidden from each other's outside lives. As he sat now, picking the chicken out of his dinner and feeling as lonely as a ball bobbing on an ocean, he decided enough was enough. He'd wallowed and stared into his soul enough this week and it was time to stop. He knew in his heart that he couldn't guarantee it wouldn't happen again but he'd have to live with that fear.

Tate picked up his mobile and took a deep breath as he called Clay's number. It was answered almost immediately.

"Hey." Clay's gentle voice was like a soothing balm on a stinging cut. "Are you okay?"

"Yeah, fine. Sitting here thinking I want to plough Vin Diesel's arse and wondering if he'd let me."

The husky chuckle from the other side of the phone perked Tate and his cock right up.

"You always have this thing for him. I'm not sure of the attraction myself." There was a garbled muttering in the background, laughter and the sound of soft music.

Tate frowned. "Am I interrupting? You sound as if you're in the middle of something." Part of him felt a little peeved that Clay was having fun without him. It was completely illogical. He'd been the one who'd kicked him to the kerb.

"I'm having dinner with Draven and Taylor at Galileo's. They knew I was down so they bought me one of Eddie's famous 'Chocolate Orgasm' desserts to get me through it." Clay's voice was matter of fact, not at all judgmental about Tate being a bit of an arsehole and pushing him away. Tate closed his eyes as a wave of guilt swept through him.

"I miss you," he murmured softly.

There was silence then, "I miss you too."

"I'd love to see you. Do you think—" Tate hesitated. "Do you want to come over later after you finish stuffing your face with pudding?" He took a deep breath and waited for Clay's response.

There was a sudden quiet and a whispered conversation in the background then it sounded like the phone was grabbed as someone came onto the line with all the subtlety of a Force Twelve hurricane.

"Tate, is that you?" Taylor's voice was slurred, and Tate sighed.

"Yes, Taylor, it's me." They'd met on various occasions and Tate really liked the wild, unconventional being that was Taylor Abelard.

"You need to stop being such a fucking prat and giving Clay gray hairs. He's a really nice guy and he's been bloody miserable and I for one—wait, Clay, what the fuck are you doing? Ouch, stop that, you bully. Draven, what the hell are you doing with that fork— fuck, that hurt, you bastard. You are *so* not getting any tonight—"

Taylor's indignant tone was cut off as he squealed loudly and there was muffled laughter on the other side, deep and amused. Tate knew it to be Draven. He'd heard that laugh often enough before at the office. Tate was also curious about Taylor's words. It sounded as if the man knew the real nature of his and Clay's relationship.

What has Clay been telling them? Has he finally confided in someone?

With a small flicker of hope in his soul, he grinned into the phone as he imagined the scenario being played out in the restaurant. Finally there was a loud scuffling noise and the next he knew, Clay was on the phone again. He sounded out of breath and rather apologetic.

"Love, are you still there? Sorry about that. I swear I haven't been bad mouthing you. Taylor came to the whole prat conclusion all by himself. He's had one B-fifty-twos too many and he's a menace to society when he gets tipsy. His mouth knows no bounds. Dray's not much better off either."

"Don't worry about it. I can see you have your hands full with those two." Tate snorted with laughter.

There was a sudden flurry of words, a loud guffaw and then Clay groaned.

"Yeah, Taylor, tell the restaurant *exactly* what your mouth does with Draven. God, Dray, shut him up will you? I don't care how. Oh, shit. I didn't think you'd actually *do* that whole 'stick your tongue down his throat' in public to keep him quiet…"

Clay sounded flustered and Tate felt better with each minute with the events being enacted on the other end of the phone. His one regret was that he wasn't there to see it himself. He broke into quiet chuckles at Clay's next mortified words.

"Oh hell, Gideon, I'm so sorry. I understand you don't need a porn show in your dining area. I promise to get these two drunken sods out of here. Just let me say goodbye to my boyfriend. Love, I'll come over once I've off loaded these two, okay? See you later. Love you."

The line went dead and Tate stared at the phone with a sense of longing. He wanted that camaraderie too. He wanted to be with Clay, in public, instead of hiding who they were to each other. He wanted to sit in a restaurant and fool around with friends. It did sound as if Clay had perhaps opened up a little about their relationship. Maybe Tate's last words about being molly coddled, spoken the night he told Clay to leave, had finally struck a chord.

It was close to ten-thirty when Clay finally arrived. There was a tentative knock at the door, almost as if he was expecting him not to answer. Tate took a deep breath. He'd had a shower, shaved and put on a clean pair of jeans and polo shirt and he was ready. The bedroom was well stocked with lube; the toys, an electro wand and torpedo plug they'd bought together at a sex fair in Manchester, had fresh batteries. He didn't think that sort of play was on the cards tonight; no, tonight he just wanted to be close to Clay—but who knew?

He opened the door and his heart beat faster at the simple fact that his lover stood there. Clay looked tired and a little frazzled, but the scent of him and the hesitant smile on his face made Tate's world a little brighter.

He reached out and pulled Clay inside, not even stopping to say anything. His mouth found Clay's, his tongue pushed inside a warm, chocolate and whisky-scented mouth and from that point on, the clock stopped. Clay's answering moan into his mouth, the way he pulled Tate's hips against his groin, the already-hardened cock Tate found pressed into his crotch; those actions spoke louder than any words.

They grappled with each other, both ravenous, each of them trying to say something in the pressure of lips on lips, the thrust of tongues, each seeking dominance, releasing soft groans as hands found skin. For Tate, it was 'Welcome Home,' 'I'm sorry' and 'I love you' all at once.

Clay pushed Tate back against the wall and pinned his arms to his sides, his mouth sucking on Tate's bottom lip. Tate heaved a shuddering sigh and gave into his lover, his body becoming pliable and surrendering to whatever Clay wanted to do with it.

"You smell like sandalwood," Clay finally murmured when his lips stopped assaulting Tate's. "Did you shower?" His pupils were dilated and there was only a thin green line around them. It was sexy as hell and Tate loved that he was the cause of it.

"Yes," he whispered. "And I fingered myself too, tried to get ready before you got here." He noted Clay's flared nostrils with a deep sense of satisfaction. The man was so turned on.

"God, Tate, I missed you so much." Clay's lips trailed a heated track down Tate's throat. "I thought you'd never call, but I didn't want to be a needy bastard and call you."

Tate's hands were finally released and they wandered down to the hardness at Clay's groin. His lover hissed as eager fingers rubbed his cock. "I missed you too. I'm sorry I'm such a prat like Taylor says; I just get so damn frustrated sometimes—" He hitched a breath as Clay bit his shoulder, pushing the shirt aside to get at the skin.

"Let's not play the blame game right now." Clay's hands were under Tate's shirt, his touch searing Tate's skin. "Let's just go to bed so I can fuck some loving into you. I was going to suggest double-Dutching but I really want to be inside you myself."

Tate's balls contracted and his cock swelled at those words. They tended to be pretty versatile in bed, giving and getting on an equal basis. What they called double-Dutching was always a firm favourite. Pushing something into Clay at the same time Tate was being filled, the fact they fucked each other with their own personal favourite toy; that was a huge turn-on for both of them. There were nights when Clay would drive him insane with it all and the constant assault on his body and his senses. And then there were nights like tonight when he just wanted to be as close to Clay as possible and feel him inside him.

He tugged Clay toward the bedroom, already set with candles flickering in the darkness and the smell of incense permeating the air. The covers were already folded back neatly to the bottom of the bed.

Clay's eyes smouldered as he looked around the room. "You had this all planned out then? Are you trying to seduce me, Mister Williams?"

Tate laughed huskily. "I did and I am. Now get your clothes off and into bed. I need to feel skin, cock and your mouth everywhere.

As for the candles—you can put them to good use later. Round two, maybe."

The shiver that ran through both his own and Clay's body at those words was anticipation. Tate enjoyed having hot wax on his skin and Clay enjoyed putting it there. There were a few other things they'd experimented with: ice against Tate's prick and balls, then rubbed on his arsehole until it froze so that Clay's warm tongue could warm him up. Another favourite was using the pulsing wand on Tate's cock, taint and balls until Tate was ready to scream with the tension before begging Clay to finish it.

Both men disrobed hastily and Tate's skin prickled in pleasurable response to the sight of Clay's heavy balls, and the erect cock curving against the muscles of his groin and stomach. A dark line of black hair ran into a neatly clipped bush above his cock and as Tate watched, his breath deepening, Clay's stomach muscles contracted as he palmed himself and looked at Tate with a wicked grin.

"Ready for this? I'm too damned horny and I can't promise this is going to be slow or easy. In fact, I think I can pretty much guarantee I'm going to pound the life out of you." His voice deepened. "Get on the bed, Tate, onto your back."

Sometimes not making love, but taking it rough and hard, was necessary. This was one of those times. Tate hastened to do as he was told. He scooted onto the mattress, lying back on the continental pillows against the wrought-iron headboard. Endorphins raced through his blood as his anticipation built, and his prickling skin screamed for Clay to touch him and anoint him with his own sweat and come. To claim him. To make things right, at least for a little while.

Clay watched with hooded eyes and slightly parted lips as Tate deliberately spread his legs, dropping them to the side so he was exposed, then gently ran his hand over the flat planes of his stomach and down toward his prick, which jutted up, proud and ready. Keeping his eyes on Clay's face, Tate stroked himself, making sure his hand swept over the head of his cock. He gasped as his calloused palm hit a particularly sensitive spot and was gratified to see Clay's cock swelling, the purple head glistening.

"You look so damn sexy like that." Clay's voice was thick with desire. "I've been dreaming about you like this. Lying there, open for me, ready to take you, be inside you."

Tate smiled lazily. "Yeah? Then you'd better get over here before I finish myself off, because it won't take long." He twisted his hand around his cock again and drew in a deep breath at the sensation.

The bed dipped as Clay got on and before Tate could even make another stroke, his wrist was gripped and pinned above his head.

"You will come when I do," Clay growled. "Just from me fucking you, you hear me?" His body covered Tate's, the feel of hot, slick skin against his frying his brain and making his insides churn.

He nodded wordlessly, loving the dominance that Clay brought to the bedroom. In Tate's career as a policeman, he'd always had to be in control. With Clay, he could lose that part of him and succumb to someone else. Tate thanked God each time he submitted like this that his enforced incarceration with Sonny Armerian hadn't taken this part away from him. He might have been bound then and had no choice about what was done to him, but with Clay, he knew there was always an out.

"I hear you," he murmured breathily. "Just fuck me already, for God's sake."

Clay's mouth covered his and his forceful kiss would have made Tate's knees buckle had he been standing up. He moaned, and his groin pushed up to rub against Clay's. God, he needed release so badly. His cock ached, his balls were tight and his arsehole waited in anticipation for Clay's breach.

From under the pillow, Clay brought out the lube. He moved back, straddling Tate's hips as he opened the cap and rubbed it onto his fingers.

"Bring your knees up," Clay murmured and Tate obliged, lifting his knees almost to his ears. Clay's face flushed in the dim light, and the look on it at seeing his lover open like that was almost Tate's undoing. The look was reverent and worshipping but also filled with pure lust. Then cool, vanilla-scented liquid was pushed into him together with Clay's fingers—two of them from the feel of it. Tate arched his back and whimpered at the feeling of being filled.

They had no need of condoms; they'd been together exclusively for long enough for each of them to commit to that. And while it was messier and they needed to change their bed sheets far more often, Tate wouldn't have given that up for anything. The heady feeling of Clay's naked cock in his arse, with its smooth heat and slickness, and the feel of Clay's semen leaking out of him afterward was manna from heaven.

He groaned as he was breached more deeply, Clay's fingers pushing in, finding that place inside him that made him see spots, that caused his body to tremble as waves of pleasure coursed through him. "Just there…feels so good. Need you in me."

Clay kissed his cheek softly as his fingers withdrew, and then his warm, hard body pressed against Tate's as he slid inside him.

Tate cried out as Clay stretched him, silken flesh pressing against his inner walls. He pushed his hips toward the welcome intrusion. Clay gasped as he sank deeper and leaned down and bit the side of Tate's neck gently, no doubt marking him.

"I missed you," Clay whispered as they moved together, lost in the sensation of each other's bodies and murmurs of need. "Thought about you every damn minute…"

His thrusts grew frenzied and Tate gripped his backside and urged him deeper still. He caught sight of Clay's face above him, sweat gleaming on his cheeks and forehead, eyes half closed as he bit his lip. His look of concentration was intense and Tate reached up and gripped his face, bringing him down for a kiss, claiming the man inside him with the possessive need borne of love.

Tate's cock was near to bursting, and he wrapped a hand around it then moaned when Clay pushed his hand away.

"No, you come just from *this*," Clay growled, "Me inside you. You've done it before; now let me see it. Think about my cock deep inside you, marking you, giving you my seed..." He leaned in to Tate's ear. "Me *fucking* you like this. Making you mine." He pushed Tate's legs back, gripping him tighter and drove even harder, to the point of near pain.

Those words and the aggressive passion with which he was being well and truly screwed drove Tate to the edge. As Clay reared back and rammed into him again, Tate managed one sly twist of his cock with his hand and climaxed. Shuddering as his body rode out his orgasm, dimly he heard Clay's shout and the warmth flooding his arse as he came too. Breath heaving with the force of his release, Tate lowered his aching legs and lay beneath Clay's heavy body. His heart pounded madly, his arse was sore and the room bore the scent of sex, sweat and Clay's unique fragrance. His lover toppled off him onto the bed and lay there beside him.

"You cheated," Clay finally muttered as he raised himself on one elbow and observed him with a smile. "Think I didn't see that little move you did when you palmed your cock?"

"Yeah, yeah; you don't miss a thing do you?" Tate wiped a strand of sticky semen off Clay's stomach, raising it to his mouth and sucking on it. Clay's eyes darkened. "Mister Hawk Eyes, that's you."

Clay chuckled. "Next time I'm going to tie your hands to the headboard so you can't touch yourself."

Tate's cock jumped a little. "*That's* no punishment," he said softly as he trailed his tongue along Clay's jawline.

Clay grinned tiredly. "Oh, yeah. What the hell was I thinking…? You love that stuff." He rolled his eyes as he settled back onto the pillow on his side, facing Tate and pulling the duvet over them both. "Time to sleep. Are you okay to talk in the morning about things?" His tone was hesitant.

Tate took a deep breath. "I guess. I know we should." He frowned. "Did you tell Draven about us? I know Taylor knows and Draven is the only common connection I can think of."

Clay was quiet for a minute before replying. "Yes. I had a rough night the night you kicked me out. I got drunk, spat my mouth off." He shrugged. "Either Taylor read his mind or Dray spilled the beans. He can't resist that man of his. But I know both of them will keep it quiet."

I don't want it kept quiet. But I'm not going there right now. Clay will be surprised enough at the next therapy session when it comes to that sensitive topic.

Under the cover, he ran a hand across Clay's stomach then turned himself into the little spoon. Clay's strong arm swung across him as he pulled him closer, his half-soft cock pressed against Tate's cheeks.

"'Kay." Soft lips brushed against the back of his head. "I hope you manage to sleep well, love. I'm glad I'm back."

Tate nodded as he closed his eyes. "Uh huh, me too." He was already drowsy and feeling safe with Clay's arms around him. Maybe the nightmares would stay away tonight.

Chapter 5

In his time in the RAF and then the SAS, Clay had faced many
dangers. He'd been thrown out of an aeroplane by a manic instructor,
kicked in the head by a rogue donkey in Afghanistan, been
submerged in below-freezing waters, been shot at, stabbed and
beaten more times than he cared to remember. He'd encountered
crazies intent on his destruction, drunk more alcohol than was
healthy for him and killed many men and a woman. The latter had
been a lady (and he admitted he used that term loosely) hell bent on
slitting his throat during a deep cover operation in Prague. Nothing,
however, had ever prepared Clay for the relationship skills and
patience that he needed to manage the volatile being that was Tate
Williams.

Dr. Jakes smiled at him. "Something on your mind, Clay? Want
to share?"

Clay smirked. "Your last question reminded me about our
school years together." He waggled a finger in Tate's face. "Even as
a teen, he was a damn handful. When he was thirteen, he was the
first one of us to come out." He chuckled and saw Tate grin at the
memory. "He made this huge, six-foot-long, two-foot-high banner at
the mock junior prom and hung it across the dessert table. It said,
'Yeah, I'm a fucking fruit. Get over it.'"

Both men sniggered loudly. This was their third session as a
couple and Clay really believed that it was helping them both
manage Tate's behaviour and moods. He'd been giving a lot of
thought to Draven's words too. He knew he needed to tackle it
sooner rather than later, despite his fear for his lover's safety.

Dr. Jakes raised her eyebrows at Tate. "Confrontational much?"
she said with a warm smile.

Tate laughed. "That's what happens when you call me fag and
queer. I had to hit back somehow."

Clay prodded Tate's arm. "You hit back in more than that way.
You beat the crap out of those two jocks who called you that because
they saw you kissing that boy in the schoolyard. Then you decorated
the town and got caught, leading to more damn trouble."

Clay had been unhappy with that for two reasons. Firstly, that
the boy Tate had deep- Frenched wasn't Clay. It had been some

geeky straight schoolmate who had dared Tate to kiss him and everyone knew you didn't dare him because…well, it was just downright stupid. He was Tate, for God's sake.

Secondly, he'd been concerned for Tate for fighting back and injuring the two other boys. Tate had been suspended while the school board investigated the incident. Luckily, one of the teachers sympathetic to Tate had seen the event unfold and confirmed that Tate hadn't started it.

Tate scowled. "So I went on a bit of a binge to celebrate my newly declared homo status. Some of those shop owners had no sense of humour." He grinned. "All I had to do was clean it up. I got off with a caution."

Graffiti was an art talent that Tate still possessed. He'd go off by himself occasionally when he needed solace, and Clay had no doubt that somewhere in the neighbourhood there'd be a new piece of art on the city streets.

Clay glanced at the doctor, who appeared highly amused by the stories. "Less than a year ago, we went to Croydon and Tate felt the need to spray the police station with his genius. We were rather drunk, and it was three in the morning. It seemed like a good idea at the time. I was shitting bricks that we'd get caught."

Tate laughed loudly. "Yeah, one of the senior detectives at the station was an ex-lover of mine and he was a complete prat and a cheating arsehole. It was payback time."

Both of them grinned at each other, and Clay guessed they were both remembering the two-foot-high rendition of a backside and an arsehole painted on the station wall. It had been painted over quickly after discovery but they still chuckled when they drove past the wall.

Natalie Jakes nodded and leaned forward, her eyes observing Tate carefully. "You guys sound like a right pair. Well matched, I'd say," she remarked drily.

Then she got back to business. "So, Tate. The halfway house."

Clay knew Tate had a temper. He'd been on the receiving end himself more than once. Now, as he watched his man scowling fiercely across the table at his therapist, he hoped Dr. Natalie Jakes had bigger balls than his lover. She was going to need them.

"Yeah, I heard you on that. You want me to spend time at a kid's halfway house. Why?"

Clay tried to hide his smile at Tate's ferocious snarl. His partner actually loved kids, and in his career as a policeman, he'd always been the first to volunteer for the school talks and Career Day opportunities. Tate just simply had to challenge everything. It was the nature of the beast.

Clay sat back and waited in anticipation for Dr. Jakes's reply.

The psychologist mock-frowned at Tate who frowned back. "It's a great halfway house, for abused and troubled teens. The owner, Randall Pierce, is a friend of mine. He thinks the young people would benefit from an older role model, someone who knows what they've been through and can identify with them. You wouldn't need to tell them your whole story. Just talk to them, make them understand you know where they're coming from. Tell them some stories about when you were a policeman."

"How? I wasn't a troubled teen," Tate said mulishly. "And I wasn't... abused. I was tortured by a psycho in the course of my job." His voice lowered and he glanced across at Clay quickly then back to the doctor.

Clay had heard the slight hesitation in Tate's voice when he said he hadn't been abused, and from the look on her face, so had his therapist. Her eyes darkened and she threw a wary glance at Clay, whose stomach clenched at what he suspected Tate wasn't telling anyone.

Dr. Jakes leaned forward, a sympathetic glint in her eye. "These kids suffer from PTSD, Tate, and that, my friend, you definitely have in common with them."

Clay hitched a breath. His boyfriend wouldn't like that statement.

Dr. Jakes forestalled Tate's next words as Clay had no doubt he'd try and refute that statement. "And we've had this conversation before. You might not acknowledge it, but it's a fact."

Tate muttered under his breath and leaned back in his chair, long jeans-clad legs stretched out in front of him. He turned and glared at Clay, who wisely kept quiet.

She warmed to the subject. "I think it would be good for you to see these kids, interact with them. We aren't talking sexual abuse only, we're talking actual physical and mental harm, and some of these children are as young as eight years old. I think you have the empathy to help them. At the same time, it would be good for you to see what they've been through. It might give you all some perspective." She smiled at Clay. "Clay tells me you're good with kids. They respond to you. So one day a month isn't going to kill you, is it? I'm sure the boss will give you the time off."

Clay nodded, trying to keep the grin from his face. "Oh, I think I can safely say the boss will be happy to give Tate some leave."

He heard a snort and what sounded suspiciously like 'Fucking Jezebel' from Tate. But it looked like he wasn't going to argue anymore and was resigned to the suggestion. Her next words threw him.

"And Clay—it's time you and Tate started being open about your relationship, with other people and in public." Her tone was even but Clay heard the steel in it.

Clay's eyes widened as he stared at her. "Where the hell did that come from?" He felt a stir of resentment. Even though he'd reached the same conclusion himself, and had been meaning to discuss it with Tate, he was irked at being blindsided. He suspected ruefully that this was the real reason for his last attendance at the three sessions he'd been to.

Tate shifted in his chair and then raised troubled eyes to Clay's. The two men stared at each other. Clay waited for Tate to go first.

"I need you to let go a bit, Clay," Tate said quietly. "We've talked about this, so it's no real surprise. I don't want to be protected or kept secret. I need to feel—" his voice caught. "I need to believe you still see me as strong enough to look after myself despite what I went through. You need to have confidence in me that I know what's best for me."

Dr. Jakes watched their exchange with narrowed eyes. She twirled her pen around in her fingers as she observed them.

Clay reached over and took his hand. "God, baby, I know that. You're the strongest man I know. You are without doubt my damn hero."

Tate's eyes softened. "Then trust me to be that hero, Clay. Stop worrying that the bad guys out there are going to get me again, and be the man I love. *That* I can live with. But being sheltered, having you see me as half a man—that I can't do anymore." He swallowed and his fingers tightened in Clay's grasp.

Clay's jaw dropped. "Half a man? I have *never* thought that of you." His heart beat faster. "You're my world, Tate, my everything.

I can't bear the thought of someone hurting you again; that's why I keep us a secret."

"And therein lies the problem, Clay." Dr. Jakes's soft voice echoed in Clay's eardrums. "This isn't about you. It's about Tate. He needs to feel you still see him as the man he was before Armerian got hold of him. Not someone to be wrapped up in cotton wool. It's hindering his healing process."

"I realise that," Clay said gruffly. "It's all I've been thinking about for the last damn week myself."

Tate stared down at their clasped hands then raised anxious eyes to Clay's. "I understand your fear, I do. But I can look after myself. I was an undercover agent for Christ's sake. I failed at that once. But I won't fail again." His jaw jutted in determination. "Have you ever thought that I feel the same way about you? That you go off to work, might get involved in dangerous situations and you might not come home one night?" His voice cracked. "I would fall apart if anything happened to you. But I don't expect you to do anything different because of who you are and what you do. Well, this is who I am, Clay. You need to deal with it." He swallowed. "We spend so much time together, sleep at each other's houses. Anyone who really wanted to hurt me through you would put two and two together anyway. What you're doing means jack shit in keeping me safe. They'd know how much you mean to me and me to you just by looking at us. That's why I get mad, because you don't see it that way."

Clay was dazed. He didn't want to admit it right now but he knew exactly what Tate was talking about. He *had* been hiding his head in the sand, pretending no one would figure it out if they kept the semblance of not being in a relationship.

As for danger to him—Clay *had* been getting some threatening phone calls recently telling him something nasty was going to happen to him if he didn't back off a certain missing-person investigation his team was working on.

His agency and the police were now involved because it looked like there was a tie-in to a case they were working on, involving toxic waste being dumped illegally in an abandoned quarry in Oxfordshire. The scenario had the potential to be similar to the Monsanto scandal in Wales a while ago. Clay had been down at the police station with Tate's nephew Rick at the time, who'd convinced

Clay to file a report on the threats, 'just in case.' Clay had done so to placate Rick but he didn't really think anything would come of it, or anything would happen to him. He got threatened all the time.

Tate didn't know about the threats and now wasn't the time to tell him.

Clay nodded jerkily. "I get it. I'm sorry—"

Tate leaned forward and placed a warm finger on his lips. "Don't ever be sorry for trying to keep me safe. Just turn it down a notch. Let *us* breathe."

Clay reached up and kissed the hand at his mouth. He nodded. "I'll try. Do you want me take out an ad in the newspaper saying 'Tate Williams and Clay Mortimer are in a relationship, having mind-blowing sex and will continue to do so for the foreseeable future'?" The thought definitely gave him a buzz. He wanted nothing more than to tell the world Tate was his, but his fear had held him back. But now was the time to make it right.

The wide smile on Tate's face at his attempt at humour made the world a brighter place. "I think we can give the banners a miss," he grinned as he leaned back in his chair. "But we can go out and do it with graffiti if you like. That would be cool. I miss doing that now I'm supposed to be 'respectable.'"

His body was more relaxed and Clay wondered if that capitulation on his part was all it had needed to achieve that. If so, he felt a real prat for not listening to Tate sooner.

Dr. Jakes grinned at him. "There. That wasn't too bad, was it?" she said jokingly. "And as for that graffiti thing you do, Tate…" She pressed her hands over her ears. "I heard nothing."

Both men smiled sheepishly. She leaned forward and slid a piece of paper across her desk. "This is the address of the home. It's called Castaways and it's in Camden. Randy is expecting you, so just call him and set up when you fancy going in." Her face grew serious. "I really think this could help as part of your therapy, so be very aware that this course of treatment is mandatory. If I get a call from Randy asking me why you haven't called yet, I shall be displeased." She grinned wolfishly. "And you won't want that, trust me."

Clay had no doubt that statement was true. Natalie Jakes's reputation was legendary. She might only be a slim, five-foot-five, bespectacled, red-haired woman but she had determination and grit.

She'd been recommended to him by a former colleague of Clay's in the SAS who confessed she'd had him sobbing like a baby in his own session.

She looked at her watch. "Time's up, gents. Go home, fuck each other's brains out and let off some steam."

Both Tate's and Clay's mouths dropped open.

The therapist smiled wickedly. "What? I watch gay porn. It's hot. I read gay romance books too. So shoot me." She shrugged. "Are you going to report me for unprofessional behaviour? You know I'm not all that conventional at the best of times."

Clay guffawed at that understatement. Tate grinned but there was an element of wide-eyed surprise in them at her words.

"Doctor's orders, love," Clay said with a leer. "I think she has something there, with fucking as therapy."

Tate's tanned cheeks pinked up. Clay shook his head. Tate could shoot the wings off a gnat at a hundred paces, talk dirty with the best of them and had some kinks Clay wouldn't ever reveal to anyone, but discussing his sex life with his doctor got him all embarrassed.

"Thanks, Doctor." Tate held out a hand and shook hers. "So, same time next week? And I'll give Randy a call. I promise."

They left the office, and on the drive home as Clay manoeuvred his Audi through the city traffic, little was said. Tate had reached over and laid a hand on his thigh as Clay drove. The solid contact had warmed Clay. He felt that somehow today they'd turned a corner—one that he had probably been guilty of delaying with his paranoia. This thought rankled all afternoon and night, even when he climbed into bed that night at his home where Tate was staying over.

His partner was reading a Norman Mailer book called *The Faith of Graffiti*. It was a well-worn copy that he browsed through every time he wanted to read something familiar. Seeing it, Clay instinctively looked at the far wall of his bedroom where a painting hung. It was a large, square, silver-framed picture of Tate's tag signature. It was a simple *TW* in some funky script, in bright red, because that was Tate's favourite colour.

Tate had never understood Clay's reasoning for having the print done and framing it. Yet in Clay's head, this was a unique portrait of everything Tate Williams stood for. Unconventional. Brave. Quirky. Headstrong. Fearless. Not to mention his whole 'stick it to the man' philosophy, which was contradictory to him being a detective. And *so* Tate.

Tate looked up at him and laid the book down on his side table. His chest was bare, the covers pooled at his waist. "Work stuff finished for the night? And it's not even midnight," he said teasingly.

Clay took a deep breath as he slid into bed, clad in his sleep boxers. "I finished work stuff a while ago. I was busy with personal stuff."

Tate nodded. "Bills and things? Hope you paid the electricity bill. I put that load of fresh fish from the market we went to earlier in the freezer. You don't want that going off." His nose wrinkled.

Clay turned to face him and reached out a hand to idly stroke the bullet-hole scar on Tate's chest. "No. I called home actually. Spoke to Mum and Dad."

Percy and Angela Mortimer still lived in the neighbourhood where he and Tate had grown up. They'd been neighbours to Tate's parents, Sam and Rachael. Tate's folks were now deceased; his dad had a heart attack when Tate was in his twenties, and his mother died four years later from a brain aneurysm. Clay had been devastated when he'd learnt that. Tate didn't talk about them much, but Clay knew his own folks had been there for Tate when Clay had been off roaming the world. They were exceptionally fond of Tate and his big sister Lucy.

"Oh?" Tate's eyebrow lifted. "How are they? Still looking to win Garden of the Month?" he snorted. As youngsters, he and Clay had spent a lot of time toiling in the garden trying to win the coveted village trophy.

"They're fine. I, ermm, I told them about you. About us being together."

Tate stilled. "As in *together*-together?"

Clay nodded. He lay back on his pillows and crossed his hands under his head as he stared at the ceiling. "It was a bit of a let-down actually. They said they knew. Something about how I looked at you whenever you walked into a room." He rolled his eyes. "I didn't know I was that transparent. But they didn't want to bring it up until I did."

There was silence. He risked a look at Tate, whose face was glowing, his eyes shining.

"You really mean to keep your promise, don't you?" he whispered. His hand came out and brushed a strand of hair of Clay's forehead. "I know this isn't going to solve everything, Clay. I'm still going to struggle; there's no quick fix. But it means a lot to me that you listened today."

"I just wish I'd done it sooner," Clay said sadly. "I feel like a dick for making you feel less than you are. That was never my intention. I'm a man. I should have understood how you felt being treated like a kid. I just wanted to keep you safe."

Tate shifted over to run his fingers down Clay's chest and push the covers down past his hips, revealing his already semi-erect cock.

"Oh, yes, indeed," Tate murmured as his lips traced down from Clay's hardening nipple and trailed down his skin. "You are definitely a man." He gave Clay a wicked smile, his eyes heated under long lashes. His fingers curled around the base of Clay's aching hard–on. Clay gasped as Tate licked the tip and then licked a long, wet path down the underside. "And I need to test out the doctor's advice about fucking being therapy. So hold on to your balls, honey, because you are about to get the ride of your life."

Clay choked down a laugh even as his body thronged with sensation at what Tate was doing to his dick. "I'd rather *you* held onto my balls, actually. Oh, God, yes. Just like that…"

Clay closed his eyes and braced himself.

Chapter 6

Tate stood in front of a large house in the leafy suburb of Camden and gazed at the building perched at the top of the stone steps. It looked innocent enough—an old Victorian house, similar to Clay's, built of red brick with a white door. The sign bolted to the left of the ornate iron gate read simply 'Castaways.' He grunted moodily as he walked up the steps to the front door then pressed the bell.

The house was on a busy street, the hustle and bustle of traffic behind him drowning out the sound of any bell that may have rung inside. He waited. It had been a week since he'd promised to make it down here, and although he'd kept his promise to Dr. Jakes, he wasn't really in the mood.

After a minute, the door swung open. A harassed-looking woman in around her mid-forties or so stood there, dishcloth in hand and a weary smile on her face.

"Yes? Can I help you?" She glanced quickly out into the street then her gaze swung back to his face.

He forced a smile. "I'm Tate Williams. I'm here to see Randall Pierce?"

Her face cleared. "Oh, yes. I'd heard someone was coming. I hadn't expected you so soon. I thought you were coming later in the afternoon."

Tate cleared his throat. "If it's inconvenient, I can always come back later."

Yep. Like much later.

He was grumpy; he hadn't slept well, had been restless and the remnants of his bad dream from last night still haunted him. Clay cutting the strings on the overprotectiveness a little had changed something. Tate felt more at ease and the nightmares had lessened somewhat, but they could still invade his sleep like an unwelcome guest. The other day a car had backfired and while Tate had started and his gorge had risen in fear, it hadn't caused an extreme reaction similar to the firecracker incident. He'd been able to control it.

She waved at him with the dishcloth. "Oh no, it's fine. Please come on in. Randall is around somewhere. I'll get him for you."

Tate stepped into the hallway and his ears rang as the woman bellowed out loudly. "Randy. Your guest is here."

A harried voice called out from somewhere in the distance. "I'll be there in a moment, Jen. Please show him to the lounge. Tell the kids not to bother him if they're in there. No need to scare him off before we even get started."

Tate shook his head at the fact that this Randall guy thought a few kids could scare Tate. He'd faced far greater perils.

Jen laid a hand on his arm. "If you follow me, I'll show where to wait." She motioned him over to a room on the side. "Would you like a cup of tea, or coffee?"

Tate shook his head as he followed her into the room. "No, thank you. I—" His voice cut off as he encountered a few pairs of eyes staring fixedly at him. It *was* as unnerving as hell, like something out of *Children of the Corn*. The kids, ranging in age from about seven to twelve years old observed him with the fixation of a cat about to devour a bird. Tate could now see what Randy had been warning Jen about.

"Uhm, hi," he proffered as he waved a hand in their direction and cursed Natalie Jakes for putting him in this situation. The youngest looking kid in the group was a podgy, dark-skinned boy with black, shining eyes, and cornrow hair. He barked at Tate.

Tate blinked in confusion at the shrill 'Woof' emanating from that stocky little frame.

Jen tut-tutted. "Now, Damian, stop that nonsense. You know you're not a dog, sweetheart." Her eyes narrowed fiercely at the others. "No matter what this lot tells you."

The room broke into sniggers as the kids all looked around at each other with sly grins. Damian smiled too, and sidled over to Tate with what looked a half-eaten string of red liquorice. He held it out solemnly to Tate who reached for it with some trepidation.

He held it uncertainly and caught Jen's eyes. She shrugged apologetically.

"I think he wants you to eat it. You don't have to, though. I mean, I don't know where it's been."

Tate nodded, and swallowed. Then he took a deep breath and shoved the liquorice into his mouth. He chewed on it—it did taste a little gritty—then gave a thumbs-up to Damian.

"Very nice," he managed to say after he swallowed what tasted to him like something out of the garbage. Tate hated liquorice.

Damian's face lit up and he nodded. He woofed again and went back to the group, who now had dropped their degree of intense observation and looked a lot more relaxed. Tate started when someone spoke behind him. It was a warm voice traced with laughter.

"Guys, stop messing with Mister Williams. He's here to see Randy, not eat your leftover yucky sweets."

Tate turned and hoped he managed to hold back the shock at seeing the face of the young man behind him.

"There you are." Jen sounded relieved. "I'm going to let young Jackson here be your host, Mister Williams. I'm sure that Randall will be with you in a moment. It was lovely meeting you." She waved her cloth at him once again and disappeared out of the room.

Tate was left facing a young man with the visage of a stricken angel. His skin was creamy porcelain, with a shock of thick, unruly blond hair curling above it. His face was pitted with small, silver scars and a few deeper pockmarks. Both of the young man's eyes were milky blue orbs floating in a picture of flawed beauty. Jackson held himself straight, his slim frame proud as he stared at Tate with a smile that radiated warmth and light.

He stepped forward without hesitation and held out a hand to Tate. "Hi. Call me Jax—with an x." He grinned, revealing straight, white teeth. "I help Randy out with stuff here."

Tate noticed Jax's chin tilted up when he spoke, and his eyes looked down, as if he was trying to see out from under his eyelids. It was a little disconcerting.

Tate shook the hand, which gripped his firmly. "Call me Tate. Pleased to meet you, Jax. It must be a pretty full-time job that, especially taking care of these ones," he waved at the now chattering group, "I imagine they're quite a handful." He stopped, wondering whether Jax could actually see the hand gesture through those damaged eyes. The teen had come into the room without any white cane or support so Tate assumed he had *some* vision.

Jax smiled. "I'm not totally blind," he confided. "I don't see well, but I can make things out, especially when I'm about to hit a wall, or a dumpster or something. I just need the right angle to get a little vision." He snorted softly. "I've done the dumpster-bashing thing before, so now I'm a bit more careful."

There was no self-pity in his tone, simply a wry awareness of his shortcomings. Tate's heart ached for such maturity and self-deprecation in one so young. He also wanted to maim whoever had done this to Jax. He'd no doubt this had been no accident but a deliberate, wilful act of violence.

Jax moved forward slowly until he stood in front of the other kids. He tilted his face upwards, his chin rising. "Right, you lot, bugger off and get outside. It's lovely out, so go and play and I'll call you when it's time for lunch."

Damian stepped forward and hugged Jax around the legs. "'Kay, Jax. I hope it's spag bol, 'cause I love that stuff."

Jax ruffled the top of his head. "It's macaroni cheese, not spaghetti Bolognese. Maybe Vicky will make that for you tomorrow. Now scarper, you lot. Mr Williams needs to speak to Randy."

The group ran out of the room, calling to each other. One child remained behind. She

came forward and touched Jax's arm. She was thin and pale with sunken brown eyes, and was no more than about ten years old.

Jax turned his head to look down at her. Tate noticed he was very careful with every move he made, his actions deliberate and slow. "You okay, Lucy?" His voice was soft. "Do you want to go outside or would you prefer to sit here and read?"

Lucy shook her head. When she spoke, Tate's stomach clenched. Her voice was strangled, hoarse, as if her throat didn't work properly.

"No. I'll go play with the others. Krispin hid my book. Can you ask him to give it back, please?"

Jax nodded. "I'll speak to him. He's just having fun, you know that, right? He's just teasing you."

Lucy's lips tightened. "I just want my book back. It's the one you gave me."

Jax's expression softened. "I promise to get it back for you." He ran a hand over the girl's lacklustre hair. "Maybe later you can wash your hair? Jen will help you look all pretty."

Lucy's eyes widened. "With apple shampoo? I like that smell." She smiled slightly and left the room.

Jax sighed, a deep, heartfelt sigh that seemed to come from the very depths of him. Due to the damage to his eyes, Tate couldn't see much expression in them but Jax's sad face spoke volumes. Tate didn't want to pry just yet; he was starting to think he'd rather *not* hear the stories behind each of these seemingly tragic individuals.

Just then there was a loud noise behind them and Tate turned to see a short, portly, bearded man bustle into the room bearing a tray of tea and biscuits. He smiled at Tate as he set the tray down on the small oak table in the middle of the room.

"Mr Williams? I'm Randy. It's lovely to meet you. Natalie's told me all about you." Tate's startled glance must have unnerved him because he continued hastily. "Oh, nothing confidential, of course, she'd never breach patient/doctor confidentiality. She shared just enough to make me curious." His wide grin would have put the Cheshire Cat to shame. "Please, have a seat, and I'll play mother. Jax, are you joining us?"

Jax shook his head. "Thanks, but I've got some studying to do." His mouth twisted. "I have an exam soon." His pale blue eyes turned towards Tate. "Nice meeting you, Tate. Hope to catch up with you soon."

Randy reached over and grasped Jax's shoulder. "Thanks, lad. Don't overdo the studying. Remember to break often, and give your eyes a rest."

Jax made a moue. "Thanks, *Dad*." He chuckled. "I promise I'll be careful."

He gave one last affectionate look at Randy and left.

"That young man is an inspiration," murmured Randy. "He's one of the bravest people I know." He glanced at Tate. "I'm sure you're dying to know everyone's story and find out why you're here, and I have to confess, I'm anxious to find out yours too." He began to pour strong tea into large mugs. "Natalie told me she thought you could help these youngsters and vice versa."

Tate blew air out. "I'm not sure how I'm supposed to help them, but I'm all ears." He poured milk into his tea. "Natalie thought this would help me." He shrugged. "I'm not sure what she hoped me to get out of it."

"That woman works in mysterious ways," Randy chuckled. "I've given up trying to understand women, and I've been married to Jen for almost twenty years."

Tate nodded his agreement and sat back. "So what's Jax's story?" The man had sparked a fierce protectiveness in him and he wanted to find out more.

Randy nibbled on a biscuit as he sat back, mug in hand. "Jax has been with us for just over two years. He was fifteen when he arrived.

He was part of a loving family, with a very privileged background and a father with an obscene amount of money. Sounds idyllic, doesn't it?" His face darkened. "Except Jax had an older step-brother called Terrence who wasn't right in the head. Terry was mean, cruel and made Jax's life a misery." He bit down savagely on his biscuit. Tate blinked at the act of aggression towards an innocent cookie.

"Jax's birth mother died when he was twelve and his father remarried a year later. Without going into detail, Jax lived in a state of hell, being picked on, harassed and beaten. His father refused to see what was going on. He travelled a lot. One night it went too far. Terry came into the house while everyone was out. He was high on something. He found Jax in his bedroom—Jax says he'd been asked to put some laundry in there by his step-mum and he'd forgotten to do it earlier—and he beat Jax almost senseless for being in his room."

He put his mug down on the table as Tate listened in horror. "Jax's dad is some megastar photographer and had his own photographic lab out the back, in the garage. Terry went out there, picked up a container of some fluid Jax's dad was using for the photo development and took it back inside." His tone was grim. "The fluid contained some sort of acid. He threw it into Jax's face while he lay there bleeding on the floor with broken ribs, internal bleeding and a bad concussion. Then he left." Randy heaved a deep sigh.

Tate gasped in horror. He might have been tortured and beaten himself but the thought of someone that young being subjected to the same pain and misery he'd experienced was horrific.

"Christ. What happened then?"

"Luckily, two things helped him keep some of his sight and negate the damage. His eyes were closed at the time because he'd been beaten half unconscious. But unfortunately it's a natural reaction to open your eyes when something splashes in your face and it didn't save his sight altogether. Secondly, the housekeeper had come back to check on the oven; she was one of those OCD individuals who thought she'd left it on.

She heard his screams and had the presence of mind to flush his eyes out with soda water or milk or something, and called nine-nine-nine. It took Jax months to recover and he's also had a lot of plastic and eye surgery. What you see today is worlds apart from what he looked like straight after the attack." He sighed. "He sees better when he tilts his head up apparently. If he looks at you straight on, it's all black and he can't see shit. It's a bit of a quirky mannerism but it works for him."

Tate was speechless. "Where's his family now? Why is he here instead of with them?"

Randy's face saddened. "Terry was arrested and because he was over eighteen—just—he got a prison sentence for grievous bodily harm. I don't know whether he's still inside or not. Jax's dad passed away about three months after the incident—a heart attack. Jax was still in the rest home at the time, having all the recuperative surgery. His step-mother sold the house, packed up and left. No one knows where she went. Jax was an only child so he had no one else. He did have a trust fund though, a good one that paid for everything and became his when his father died. It's administered through his father's lawyers and Jax becomes complete custodian of it when he's twenty-one."

Tate still wasn't clear. "If he has all that money… no offence, but why is he here, in a halfway house? Shouldn't he have his own home with a guardian and doctor at his beck and call?"

Randy's eyes lit up. "You'd think that, wouldn't you? We met at the hospital he was in. Jen and I were visiting another child, we got talking to Jax and over the months we became friends. When he heard what we did for a living, Jax asked if he could come and stay here and help us. The doctors said it would be good for his recovery, to feel useful, and if that's what he wanted, then let him."

He picked up another biscuit. "He's just never left. He's part of the extended family really. He's a stubborn little blighter, extremely independent and intelligent indeed." He popped the whole biscuit in his mouth and Tate watched, fascinated, as his muzzled jaw moved up and down.

He finally drew his gaze away. "What's he studying?" Tate asked curiously.

"He missed some school because of the attack, but he caught up and now he's doing his A-Levels in psychology via distance learning with a local college. He has special software—non-visual desktop access or NVDA—set up on his PC which he can use when he doesn't want to strain his eyes too much. The last thing we need is the last remaining vestige of sight he has disappearing altogether, so we're quite strict in trying to enforce his eye rest sessions. The college has been good about bending over backward for him, even given him some textbooks in Braille, which he can read. Plus he attends a couple of workshop sessions every month so it gets him out of the house."

Randy's eyes shadowed. "He used to be a promising young artist, but he hasn't picked up a paintbrush since. He was also involved in music and played piano; he has a real creative streak. Now he doesn't go out much and has no real friends his own age. It does worry me. He insists he's fine, but I wonder. Sometimes he gets this look…" His voice tailed off and Tate waited to see what *look* this might be. When Randy didn't continue he simply nodded.

"It's a damn tragic tale for one so young. Makes mine seem paltry in comparison…" Tate hesitated at the wicked glint in Randy's eyes and the sudden knowledge that he'd had been played. That was *exactly* the reaction he knew that Dr. Natalie Jakes had been looking for.

He raised his cup of tea to Randy. "Touché," he acknowledged. "Therapists are manipulative bastards, aren't they?"

The other man chuckled loudly. "Tell me your story then."

And Tate did. Not all of it, admittedly. There were aspects of his torture at Armerian's hands that he'd never revealed, to either his therapist or Clay. It was too intimate, too shaming and he'd probably go to his grave with his secret. When'd he finally finished his story, and Randy had eaten half of the packet of biscuits and drunk most of the pot of tea, Tate felt…purged. It had felt good sharing it with someone who wasn't close to him like Clay or someone who was trying to heal him. Randy simply listened.

"Shit, that's some pretty heavy stuff," Randy said, drawing a breath between his teeth. "Thanks for telling me. I'm sorry you went through that." He leaned back in his chair and gave a soft burp, then smiled apologetically. "You can certainly empathise with some of our kids here, even though your story is vastly different. Damian— he was sexually abused by his uncle for years. Lucy—," his voice grew quiet. "She was kept in a basement for close to three years by her folks. They thought she was evil because she burnt her backside on an open electric fire and they said the burn looked like the mark of the devil. Her father tried to strangle her and damaged her vocal chords. They were religious nutters. Luckily for her, one of the kids of the new next-door neighbours was a little thief. He climbed into the basement window, came out pretty quickly and told his folks about the 'weird kid' living in the basement. They told the authorities."

Tate shook his head in disbelief at the stupidity and ignorance of the human race. "What the hell is wrong with people?"

Randy shrugged. "Human beings can be the worst sort of cruel. Krispin was physically abused by his father from an early age; Cathy is six and was abandoned when she was three when her folks found out she was deaf…they wanted a perfect child and she didn't fit the bill. So they left her with a sister who was a drug addict and who didn't treat her well." He cleared his throat. "The only good thing is that they all found their way here, and are relatively stable and happy. Jax contributes to that. They love him."

"I've only just met him and even I can see how special he is." Tate agreed. "He has this calming effect, this light about him."

"That's our Jax." Randy said proudly. "I know one day he'll have to leave us and that will be a sad day when he does, but until then we're fortunate to have him." He grimaced. "Don't get me wrong, he has his bad days. Then he hides in his room and won't talk to anyone. Not even the kids can get him out of his funk. But those episodes are few."

Tate spent another half an hour talking to Randy. When he finally left that afternoon, he called Clay. He planned to let him know he was on his way to his house and he'd pick up dinner and wait for him there.

Clay answered. He sounded a little preoccupied. "Mortimer."

"Wow, that's a bit brusque, isn't it? What if I'd been a client?" Tate said in amusement.

Clay chuckled. "Sorry, I've been working from home this afternoon and was in the zone. It didn't even occur to me check who was calling. How did your visit go?"

Tate was pleased he'd get to see Clay sooner. "I can tell you I have much more of an appreciation for the work that the halfway house does."

Tate crossed the street to his car, an aging VW Golf, and clicked the key fob to open the door. "I think this whole visit was orchestrated to show me that there are others worse off than me. Randy even got me to agree to go back and give a talk to the youngsters on being a policeman." He grinned as he got into the driver seat. "I think that damn doctor was trying to give me a new perspective on things. She's one sneaky lady. She might even be in your league, my maestro of manipulation."

Clay's husky laugh went straight to Tate's dick. "Yeah? I'll show you manipulation when you get here. Your legs over my shoulders."

Tate's dick grew harder and he groaned. "Don't do that. I'm about to drive home and a hard-on will just get in the way." He started the car and put his mobile into the Bluetooth cradle.

"You could always pull over and we can have car phone sex," his lover purred seductively. As much as Tate fancied that idea, the biscuits he'd had earlier hadn't filled him up and his stomach was growling. He intended stopping to pick up Chinese food on his way home and eat *then* go to bed with Clay.

"It's an attractive offer, but I'm ravenous, and not for cock." Clay's splutter of laughter warmed Tate's heart and he laughed. "I'll pick up some Chinese and see you in a while." He shifted gears and sped up. "Oh and I met this really incredible young man called Jax. There's just something about him that makes me want to get to know him a little bit more."

Clay's voice was a little edgy when he next spoke. "Really? Does he know you're spoken for?"

Tate's stomach tingled pleasurably at the tone of possessiveness in Clay's voice. If his man had one particular fault, it was that he was jealous as hell. Not to the point of being unreasonable, but the green-eyed monster never lurked far from his cool surface.

"No, you jealous bastard, he's only seventeen. Kiddie-bait. He's been through such a lot but he just radiates this positive energy. Remarkable kid from what I've heard. I'll tell you all about him when I get home."

"Ahh." Clay didn't sound convinced. "Okay. Could you pick me up some of that crispy chilli beef please? I could really go for that."

"Roger," Tate said as he steered his way through the traffic. "I'll see you soon."

Chapter 7

Clay put down his mobile and rubbed his chin thoughtfully. Tate had sounded upbeat, more so than Clay had expected. They'd had a couple of altercations about that particular part of his therapy. Tate hadn't been looking forward to the visit to Castaways, which had led to heated, expletive-filled arguments. One had led to hot make-up sex; the other had Clay storming off to visit Draven.

Now Clay frowned, wondering who this Jax was that had Tate all warm and fuzzy. His mobile rang again. He smiled, thinking it was Tate, and didn't even bother to check the caller ID.

"Hi love, haven't they got any chilli beef then? I'll settle for something sweet and sour, you choose."

A loud snort of laughter blasted his eardrums. "Much as I like you, Clay, I have no intention of giving you anything sweet or sour. I'll leave that to Tate."

Clay chuckled at the sound of Rick's voice. "You cheeky little blighter. To what do I owe the pleasure of this call?"

Rick sighed heavily. "Sometimes I wish I'd never got that promotion to Sergeant. Now I have to do all sorts of stuff I didn't have to do as a constable. Which includes attending some sort of black-tie event and I don't have a tuxedo. I happen to know Tate hoards all his old ones in one of your cupboards. I wondered if I could borrow one; I'm sure I'll find one to fit. I haven't been able to get hold of him, and I'm in the area, so I wondered if I could pop in and rummage."

Clay snorted. "Sure, if you think you can navigate the horror that is Tate's closet. It's all cut-off jeans and sleeveless, tatty tee shirts that he can't bear to part with because they're 'comfortable.'" Tate's flat didn't have much space and Clay's home had four bedrooms—plenty of spare capacity, which meant he'd inherited a lot of Tate's *junk*.

Clay frowned as he focused on Rick's other comment. "You can't get hold of him? I spoke to him just a minute ago."

Rick's voice was wry. "Clay, don't go worrying. He's probably engrossed in conversation with Mister Yung at the takeaway. You know how they love to yack." There was the sound of scrabbling and a muttered curse then Rick came back on the line, sounding a little breathless. "Sorry about that. Some kid ran past and knocked me. I nearly dropped the phone. Okay, I'll see you in a while then."

Clay's mobile went silent and he laid it back on the table.

He wondered whether to call Tate again and find out if everything was okay. Part of him wanted to do it right now, the other, the bit that had promised his partner he'd stop being so protective, said a firm *leave it alone*.

So Clay chose to make some more business calls, mess around with some paperwork and ignore the tight feeling in his stomach that meant he was worried. When Tate walked in half an hour later, bearing fragranced bags of food, Clay was relieved.

"Got your beef," Tate announced as he threw his jacket over the chair back and disappeared into the kitchen. There was the sound of packets rustling and plates being pulled from the cupboard. Clay followed his lover into his kitchen and stood watching as Tate busied himself arranging food on plates.

"Smells good. By the way, Rick's popping over. Something about wanting to borrow one of your tuxes for some fancy do." He frowned. "I'd expected him here already." He glanced at his watch.

"Rick's coming over? Okay…" Tate's voice tailed off and he looked a little shamefaced. "Did he say anything about anything?" His tone was hesitant.

Clay looked at him. "Define *anything*." He quirked an eyebrow, curiosity spiking. Tate seemed ill at ease as he took a deep breath. "I haven't told my sister about us yet and he's been pushing me to. It's just—I know you told your folks and some of the people at work, but Lucy hasn't been around much, and every time I think I'll do it, I get distracted and Rick has been nagging me."

He rifled through the food bags with jerky movements and laid more food out on the counter. He didn't meet Clay's eyes.

Clay walked over to Tate and stayed his fiddling, his large hands grasping Tate's tightly. "Tate, it's fine. You've had a lot on your plate to deal with." He caressed Tate's cheek gently. "This isn't a race to see which one of us can tell as many people as possible."

Privately he thought the slower the news dribbled out the better. But Lucy was a bit of a firecracker and to find out she'd been one of the last to know could cause Tate a few big-sister problems. Like a slap to the side of the head.

His partner looked at him with darkened eyes filled with self-recrimination. "I made a big deal about you telling people about us but when it comes to my own sister, I just haven't gotten around to it," he muttered. "That makes me a bad person."

Clay snorted. "And when she finds out you waited so long, her wrath will be punishment enough." He grinned at the panicked look in Tate's eyes. "To be honest, I think she probably knows."

Tate's eyes widened. "Why would you say that?"

Clay leaned forward and bit Tate's earlobe, causing not only a slight yowl from him, but a shiver to run through his body.

"Because everyone tells me I look at you as if you're the whole world to me. I can't help it. It's true." He reached over and framed Tate's face, then leaned in and took his lover's mouth in a bruising kiss. The moan Tate breathed into his mouth had him hard in seconds. He never failed to love the way Tate responded to him, the feeling of his mouth on his, the eagerness with which he shoved his tongue into Clay's mouth with a fierce possessiveness.

When they pulled apart, Tate's mouth was swollen, his eyes heavy lidded. His hands had burrowed themselves inside Clay's shirt, his warm fingers on Clay's skin.

"I don't think we should do this now," Clay growled huskily. "If Rick finds us getting busy again, he'll need therapy."

His lover snorted with laughter. "Hell, yes. Last time the poor guy couldn't sleep for a week, he said." He grinned wickedly. "I still think it's because he harbours this secret fantasy about older guys and the sight of you and I going at it like rabbits turned him on."

"I heard that, you freak." The indignant voice behind them made them both swivel round. Clay saw the faint panic in Tate's eyes at the sudden interruption but it disappeared quickly when he saw his nephew smiling behind them. Rick was obviously off duty as he wore jeans and a blue tee shirt. He was carrying a cardboard carrier loaded with coffee.

Tall, broad shouldered with light blond hair and an easy grin, Rick had been *involved* with Taylor Abelard for a short time; as far as Clay knew it had been as friends with benefits, but all that had changed when Rick had met Lauren. Rick was bisexual, in his own words 'an equal opportunity employer of my dick,' but Lauren had taken hold of his heart and his senses and her red-headed beauty had captured him body and soul. They'd been together for a while now and Clay had heard marriage rumours floating about. Privately he thought that at twenty-five, they were too both young, but Rick could be stubborn like his uncle.

Tate waved a hand at his nephew. "You come bearing gifts. Good lad." He reached over and plucked a coffee out of the tray. "I understand you're scrounging for a suit?" he narrowed his eyes. "What makes you think one of mine will fit you? Better still, you really think you'll look as good in it as I do?"

He dodged Rick's slap at his head and darted out of the way.

Clay chuckled as he picked up a coffee. "He does look good in a tux." He smirked. "He looks even better out of it…"

Rick scowled. "No images, please. The sight of two guys doing the dirty isn't a problem, but when it's my uncle and his main squeeze…" he shuddered. "Not going there."

"Main squeeze?" Tate chortled. "Clay, you just got downgraded from hot-shot lover to something that comes out of a toothpaste tube."

Rick grinned and slurped his coffee. Then he flicked his eyes up to gaze at Tate.

"Have you told Mum about you and Clay yet?" His words were mild but Clay saw the effect they had on Tate.

His partner flushed. "No. I thought I'd pop over, see her tonight."

Rick nodded. "Okay. I know you've had stuff on your mind. I think she knows but she'll be as mad as hell if she doesn't hear it from you. And you know what Mum's like. *She'll* have your balls, let alone Clay having them." He sniggered then stared at Clay, a more serious look on his face. "Have you had any more death threats?"

Tate started and his expression darkened. Rick's tone faltered as he darted a guilty glance at Clay then at Tate. Clay's heart sunk and from the look on his face, Rick seemed to know he'd make a faux pas. Clay *had* told Rick that he'd let Tate know about the threats, and Clay hadn't, so Rick wasn't to blame.

Busted.

"No," he said quietly. "Nothing since the last ones."

Tate's jaw tensed. "What threats are these?" he said tightly. His mood had changed in the blink of an eye with the rapidity of a tornado changing course. PTSD was a bitch.

"It's that toxic waste case. The one you helped me with. It seems to have another element now, a missing person. About ten days ago I had a couple of threats, just the usual stuff, warning me off. The kind of threats I get because of the type of business I run."

"And you didn't tell me…why?" Tate said caustically, his eyes flashing.

Rick looked uncertainly at them both then flapped a hand. "I'm gonna go look for that tux," he stammered, and scarpered.

Clay wished he could have done the same. Tate looked thunderous.

"I didn't tell you because it was being handled. I gave a report to the cops because Rick insisted, and since then, there have been no more calls. It's gone quiet. I don't think our missing person wants to be found. If he is, he'll go to jail, maybe worse, so…" He shrugged. "It's no big deal."

Tate went ballistic. "*This* is your fucking way of not molly coddling me?" he spat at Clay. "By not telling me someone wanted to fucking kill you? And Rick bloody knows before me?"

"Rick knew because he was there when I got the call," Clay said evenly. "Not because I chose to tell him over you. Tate, you're overreacting to this." Clay's heart thudded in his chest, and a sick feeling of dread washed over him, soaking him, suffocating him.

Tate's jaw clenched as he leaned into Clay's face. "Fuck. You." He hissed and spittle hit Clay's cheek. "I thought we'd taken one step forward, Clay, but it looks like nothing has changed. You still think I can't cope with the seedy side of your life. Of *our* lives."

Clay's temper was rising now. "That's not it at all," he exclaimed. "I didn't think it mattered because they've stopped and nothing has happened to me. For Christ's sake, stop being such a bloody drama queen and listen to what I'm saying. Not everything is always about you."

No sooner were the words out than he regretted them. Tate's eyes flickered and his Adam's apple bobbed and then in one quick movement, he grabbed his leather jacket from the back of the chair where it had been resting, and strode away. The door opened and slammed on an image of Tate racing down the front steps toward the street.

Clay belatedly dashed to the front door but Tate had already crossed the street and vanished at the intersection. Clay slammed the door shut and turned and swept the flowers from the vase on the entrance table with a violent shove of his hand.

"Fuck, fuck, fuck." The petals from the fallen tulips drifted to the ground and coated the terracotta tiles with leaves of colour.

"God, I'm sorry." Rick's quiet voice invaded Clay's raging psyche. "I had no idea you hadn't told him, and I shot my mouth off. I'm so fucking sorry, Clay." Rick looked as miserable as Clay felt.

Clay shook his head tiredly. "It's not your fault. He's got a trigger temper at the best of times and this just set him off. He'll come home when he's calmed down."

"He seemed to be doing much better." Rick's tone was hopeful. "I really thought..." his voice tailed off.

"He *is* doing better," Clay said softly. "Part of the PTSD. Hair-trigger reactions. Sometimes, he gets these ideas and there's no stopping him. He hates to feel like a burden or that he's being protected." He gave a wry smile. "I thought I was doing better too at not being such a damn control freak, but I guess we both have a ways to go." He smiled at Rick, trying to reassure him, although Clay's heart wasn't in it.

His heart bled and raced through his bloodstream like acid. This whole emotional crap wasn't like him either. Tate brought out the nurturer in him, made him more vulnerable. Clay had never had these highs and lows in any other relationship before, but then he guessed you didn't often fall in love with a man who'd been kidnapped and tortured before, or who you'd worshipped since you were ten years old.

He nodded at the suit draped loosely over Rick's arms. "You found a tux then?"

Rick nodded miserably. "Yeah."

The two men were silent then Clay heaved a deep sigh. "Best get off," he murmured. "I'm sure you'd rather be with Lauren than waiting here."

Rick stared at him, his face worried. "Are you sure? 'Cos I'll wait here with you."

"No, you get off. I'll try and call him in a little while, see if he's calmed down."

Rick moved toward the door, the suit clutched in his hands. "Okay. Text me when you hear from him, though. Let me know he's okay. I'm on call tonight so I'll keep an eye on my phone."

He squeezed Clay's arm and then was gone. Clay closed the door behind him and leaned against it, closing his eyes.

Tate, you had better take care. Stupid moody bastard, just look after yourself. Come home to me.

Chapter 8

Wall to wall paint cans. Tate wandered down the aisle of his local hardware store and stared idly at the spray cans layered on the shelves. He had an itch to spray a wall somewhere, to thumb his nose at the norms of society and leave a lasting impression of his current turmoil and anger.

It had been two days since he'd raced out of Clay's house. He knew he'd overreacted. It was the nature of the beast inside him, the one that tore its teeth into his belly and lashed its stinging tail into his heart. But hearing Clay being so blasé about a threat to his own life had brought back memories of his own incarceration and near death, being imprisoned in a warehouse, chained like an animal and forced to endure indignities and pain to his body and mind that, at the time, he thought he'd never get over. Armerian had been a master at torture, both physical and psychological. Tate shuddered as he plucked cans of paint off the shelves and went to the till. He never wanted that to happen to Clay.

Clay's last words had cut him to the core.

Not everything is always about you.

Hearing them from his lover's lips had made them all the more real. He didn't want anything to be all about him; he wanted to be a whole man again and be Clay's equal. He was trying so hard, but then the whole fucking house of cards had come tumbling down around him. The thought of anyone harming Clay made him breathless with fear. Once again they'd kept in touch with text messages, and Clay's last message had been simple.

Come home.

The till assistant smiled at him and wished him a nice day as Tate handed over his cash for the paint. Tate nodded his head and tried a weak smile back.

Ten minutes later, he found himself in an old, dilapidated part of town that housed a derelict swimming pool and leisure complex. It was a haven for graffiti artists and there were normally some spraying away at the dull concrete canvases at any one time. Tate knew a couple of them; he nodded to them as he passed and made his way toward a fairly clean part of wall. Numerous pockmarked buildings dotted the quadrant of the area, all decorated with slogans and messages.

Luckily Tate looked the part to be one of the masses down here. He still had on his old sweats and a tee shirt with his leather jacket, and he always carried a beanie in his jacket pocket. It had become his method of dress when he'd been trying to infiltrate the Armerian drug operation. He'd not shaved or washed his hair and had been known to snort the occasional coke and take E, among other things. Realism was the name of the undercover game and it could save your life.

He uncapped his cans and got to work. When he painted, he got *in the zone*, ignored everything and everyone around him as he concentrated on painting his images.

By the time he'd finished, dusk had set in. He was sweaty, his hands ached and he felt a sense of achievement. He put the finishing touch to his tag and grinned as he stood back. The three-foot mural of a cartoon man hunched over in a green tee shirt, with a clockwork key sticking out of his back epitomised how he felt. Wound up, winding down, out of control, manipulated and only alive when someone turned the key. Well, that might be a little over the top but it was how he saw himself in his head.

"Meh. Not bad," said a voice from behind him. Tate swung around. A young girl of about thirteen stood there, dressed in a sloppy sweatshirt, jeans that looked too big for her and a knitted mauve cap on her head. She was scrawny, her eyes sunk deep into her face.

He scowled at her as he packed his cans back into the plastic bag. "What, you're some sort of expert?" He laid the bag on the ground.

In his days undercover on the street, he'd met plenty of these young people, the unwashed and unloved of the city with sordid histories, chips on their shoulders and dreams that had been trampled on and ground into the dirt. They expected no kindness and were as cynical as hell. He'd found the best way to deal with them was on an equal basis. Not as children. These teens had seen more pain and heartbreak than most adults.

The girl waved a hand. "I said it's not bad." She scrunched her face up and peered at the image. "Although he does look a little constipated." She giggled and Tate grinned at the sound.

"He does a bit. Like he has something stuck up his arse."

She giggled louder and then coughed, the amusement turning to hacking, chesty sounds as she turned away and hunched over. Tate watched in concern. He didn't want to invade her space or touch her. Unless she passed out or anything—then all bets about personal space were off.

Finally she stopped, but when she turned to him her eyes looked even darker, her face more pinched. "Fuck. That hurt." She wiped her sleeve over her nose. "Sorry 'bout that. Had this cough for a while. Can't seem to shake it."

Tate knew better than to ask her if she'd been to a clinic or doctor. These kids stayed away from places like those. Perhaps he could take her somewhere later, once they'd chatted. It might be worth the ask.

Instead he pulled a pack of chewing gum from his inside jacket pocket and offered her a stick. "Fancy a bit of peppermint? It might help."

She stared at him in suspicion. "How do I know you haven't drugged it or something? Guys do that all the time."

Tate's stomach clenched at the thought someone so young might be vulnerable to predators. "I'll eat one and you'll see. I promise you they're fine. I bought them earlier. See, it's a new pack." He split it open then unwrapped a piece and popped it into his mouth. The girl moved forward, watching him then silently stretched out a hand. Tate placed a stick on her palm.

A few seconds later both of them were chewing gum like cows with a cud and observing Tate's art.

"I've seen you here before," she said softly. "You did that one over there." She pointed to one of a big blue dragon surrounded by flames. "You should have made the dragon pink, it's my favourite colour. But I like him in blue, and he looks over me when I sleep. This is my favourite spot." She gestured around her. "It makes me feel at home. Plus it's a bit more sheltered from the wind."

Tate nodded even as he cringed at a cold spot in a deserted building being called home. "Yeah, I did that one. About six months ago." It had been his protest to the one tattooed on his backside. He glanced at her. "What's your name—the one you *want* to give me?" He noticed an oval pendant around her neck with the initials AK carved on them. It looked cheap but worn.

She observed him evenly for a while, her blue eyes cautious. "You can call me Lily."

Tate held out a hand. "Hi, Lily. I'm Tate. Pleased to meet you."

Her hand in his felt frail and hot. Her cheeks were pink and he thought she might have a fever from the brightness of her eyes.

"So, Tate. What's your story?" Lily sat down cross-legged on the ground. Tate followed, his legs stretched before him.

He shrugged. "Needed to let off some steam. This helps."

She grimaced. "I know how you feel. I don't have an arty bone in my body but I like to watch the artists getting busy."

"So what do you do to let off steam then?" Tate watched as a bunch of youths on the other side of the open area began pulling out spray cans and adorning the wall with bright green strokes.

Lily sniffed. "I don't. My mum used to tell me I tend to bottle stuff up inside."

"Where are your folks now then?" Tate asked nonchalantly.

She snorted. "Nice try, buster. I don't have any parents anymore."

They were quiet, both of them watching the antics of the kids, laughing and shouting as they started the picture of what looked like a giant marijuana plant.

Lily coughed again, wiping her mouth with her sleeve. She tried to move her arm quickly to her side but Tate's heart thudded when he saw bright red streaks adorning her tatty sweatshirt.

"That doesn't sound good," he said quietly. "Have you had that cough checked out at the local homeless clinic? There's one not too far away from here. If you like, I'll come with you."

I can't leave her like this.

Lily shifted as she glared at Tate with fierce eyes. "Don't need a clinic. It'll go away on its own. It won't matter much soon anyway. For either of us."

Tate tried to push. Her last words worried him. "I saw the blood, Lily. That's never a good sign. I think you should it get checked out."

Lily sprang up angrily. "Who the fuck are you? My father? I told you, I don't need any help."

She cast a scornful glance his way as he rose to his feet. "You're just like all the others, trying to get me alone so I can give you a blowjob or something or screw me. You guys are all the same." Her voice was tight but Tate heard the fear and loneliness in it. He knew those sounds well.

"Lily, I'm not wanting anything from you. I'm not into women, let alone kids."

She gave a harsh laugh. "You telling me you're a homo? You don't look like a fag."

Tate drew a deep breath. "Well, sorry to burst your bubble of what a fag looks like but yes, I'm gay. I have a boyfriend." He raised his hands palm side up. "In fact, that's the reason I'm here. We had a bit of an argument a couple of days ago." He waved around him. "This helps me focus, get over stuff. That's why I come here."

She peered at him suspiciously. "Yeah? So are you going home to him now?"

Tate shook his head. "No, I'm at my own place at the moment."

Tate would maybe call Clay in the morning. Perhaps it would lead to more frantic make-up sex. He supposed there was an upside to being a prima donna.

Lily stared at him from eyes that said she still wasn't sure about him. Tate chewed his gum, slid back down to sit on his arse and watched the kids across the quadrant and waited. Finally she sniffed and sat down beside him.

"When I first saw you painting here, I thought you were a copper. You had that air, you know? You can always tell a man in blue." She sniffed and then coughed again, her face twisting in pain. "I wondered what a man in the force would be doing down here, painting with a bunch of rebel kids. Didn't seem the sort of thing a policeman would do. Now I've met you, I *still* think you're one of them. Am I right?"

Tate glanced at her. "I was a policeman, yes. Then something happened to me and I wasn't. Short story."

Lily gave a hoarse laugh. "Did you do the dirty on someone, take a bribe? Maybe shot the wrong person in a beat down?"

Tate frowned. "You've been watching too much telly, you have. Those phrases are straight off U S television shows."

Lily flushed. "So what if they are? I sometimes sit outside the pub and watch the shows through the window if they're open. I like *Law and Order*."

Tate grinned. He rather liked this young lady.

She cocked her head. "So what happened to you that you left the force then?"

Tate stared across at the youths on the other side. "I got… hurt," he murmured. "So I was forced to leave."

"You get shot or something?" Lily asked curiously.

Tate nodded. "Yes." He wasn't rehashing his whole sorry story to someone as young as Lily.

She scowled. "You don't like talking about it, I gather. Okay, I know how that is. I don't like talking about me either." Her voice faltered. "Not much to say, really." She sounded sad and Tate looked at her.

"Why are you here, on the streets?" Tate asked quietly. "Haven't you got somewhere else you can go? Can I call someone to come and fetch you?"

Her eyes shadowed and her lips tightened. "No. I don't have anyone. I like it on the streets." Her voice was brave but the expression on her face was anything but.

Tate tried again. "I know this halfway house that takes on kids like you." He had no idea whether Castaways could take on a teenage runaway but if not, he knew other people he could contact. "I could see whether they could offer you somewhere to stay." A stray thought of Jax with his blue eyes and angelic visage flashed into his head. Despite the fact Tate didn't know Jax that well, he'd no doubt the young man would extend his compassion and help to someone like Lily.

"I said I'm fine. I don't need anyone. Will you stop fucking meddling?" Lily spat as she leapt to her feet. She looked ready to run and Tate didn't want that.

"Okay, I'm sorry. I'll stop fucking meddling. I just wanted to help." Tate raised his hands in a gesture of surrender. His heart ached for the teenager, and her stubbornness at insisting she needed no one when she so clearly did.

She scrutinised him with a sneer. "If you really want to help me, you can buy me something to eat. I like hamburgers. There's a place down the road that does good ones. Maybe bring me a Coke or something too."

Tate narrowed his eyes. It sounded like she wanted to get rid of him. His instincts told him something was wrong. He didn't remember seeing a burger place anywhere close by. It was all warehouses and old factories. He said as much and Lily rolled her eyes.

"There's a mobile burger van that gets here around this time every night, just down the street. I've seen it."

Tate was unconvinced. "Why not come with me?" he suggested. "You can see what you want."

She shook her head vehemently. "I'm not going anywhere. You want to help me, you bring me food."

Tate sighed. He still had misgivings but he couldn't hound the kid. "Fine, I'll go get you something and bring it back." He looked around. "It's getting dark. Are you going to stay here or is there somewhere else you want me to bring your dinner back to— somewhere warmer?" And safer, he thought.

Lily snorted. "Here's just fine. This is *my* place. I'll be waiting here."

Tate supposed that if he could help her with food, at least that was something. He thrust his hands into his jacket pockets and started walking away. "I'll get you some food. Be back in a bit."

"'Kay. Don't be long. I'm really hungry." Lily's voice faltered and Tate looked back at her.

She stood there, shooting him a defiant look. "What? Go already."

It took Tate over an hour to find a burger place much further down the road, order some food and then get back to the abandoned baths. Contrary to what he'd been told, there was no mobile takeaway in the area. Or perhaps there had been one but it had already left for the evening.

It was dark when he got back, the area where he'd been painting deserted. The kids painting the huge plant on the wall were nowhere to be seen. Neither was Lily.

Tate called out. "Lily? It's Tate. I have your food. Where are you?"

There was no reply, only the faint whistle of the wind as it blew across the deserted quadrant. He took out his mobile phone and used its flashlight app as a torch. There were no signs of life. Icicles trailed down his spine as his misgivings deepened. Something was wrong. As he approached a secluded area near to where he and Lily had sat, Tate smelt it. *Blood.* He was familiar with its pungent scent, both his own and that of other people. As he rounded a corner of one of the buildings in search of the young girl, his nostrils flared. The rich tang of the substance flooded his senses as aimed his phone at a motionless bundle lying in a heap of blankets against a wall.

"Lily?" he said quietly as he approached. As he got closer, he saw it *was* her—pale face, slack mouth, half-closed eyes, and he knew without any doubt that she was dead. He'd seen that look before, that dull, vacant expression that heralded death.

He tried to quell the panic in his belly, the rising sickness in his throat. Putting the now cold food on the ground and crouching down, he pulled back the red sodden blanket and gagged. Tate thought he was hardened to death, having seen junkies and gang members dead when he was undercover, but he'd never seen a young girl drenched in her own fluids, blood spread around like a fallen can of red paint. Her sweatpants had been removed and were folded neatly by her feet, only her grey and grubby daisy-printed panties covering her modestly.

His police training allowed him to dispassionately observe what looked like a fisherman's filleting knife lying next to her outstretched hand, covered in blood. From what he could see, she'd cut her femoral artery, a ragged wound marking her left thigh. Tate's first thought was that death would have been quick for Lily, although the action of cutting herself must have hurt like sin, not to mention the psychological trauma of performing such a determined act on oneself. In her other hand she clutched her pendant tightly. A tattered piece of paper peeped out from underneath the sweatpants.

Tate reached out a hand and unfolded it. The writing was scrawled, untidy and as he read it, his eyes prickled and his throat closed up.

Hey there Graffiti Man

I didn't think you'd come back. They normally don't. But if you do see this, then I'm sorry if you're the one to find me. You said you were a policeman in a past life so I guess this kind of thing is something you're used to. I like it in this spot so I needed you gone so I could do what I had to do. It's just the way it is. Don't feel sorry for us. I think we're going someplace better, some place safer.

Keep painting, you're actually pretty good.

Lily

"Oh, Lily," he whispered brokenly into the silent darkness. "Why didn't you wait for me?"

Tenderly he leaned over and brushed a strand of greasy hair from her forehead before standing up and pulling out his mobile phone. With instructions given to the emergency services, who assured him they'd be there in ten minutes, Tate sat down next to Lily's cold body and let hot tears fall.

Chapter 9

Clay was half asleep when the call came in. Groggily, he reached for his phone and became more alert when he saw who the caller was. His blood froze. Three in the morning was never a good time for a phone call.

"Tate? Is everything okay?" He sat up and swung his legs out of the bed. He was ready to move at a moment's notice. There was a silence. "Tate? You're scaring the shit out of me. Where are you?"

Finally there was a soft whisper. "I'm at the police station in Kentish Town. I'm okay. It's not me."

Clay was out of bed already, grabbing clothes and pinning the phone under his ear as he tried to get dressed. "Who is it? Is it Rick?"

Tate's voice echoed down the phone. "No, he's fine. It's—" His voice broke. "She was just a kid, Clay. And she's dead. I should never have left her. I knew something was off." A sob caused Clay's stomach to tighten and his throat to close in fear. Tate never cried. Perhaps when he was in the throes of one of his nightmares, but he'd never shed a tear during his waking hours since Armerian had gotten hold of him.

Clay cursed as he hopped around trying to get his pants on and finally succeeded. He shrugged his arms into an open shirt and slid his feet into loafers. "I'm coming down to fetch you. Hold on there, love. I'll be there soon."

There was another silence then Clay heard a soft shuddering exhaled sigh. That sound scared him more than anything. It sounded as if Tate was simply letting go. It was the sound of defeat, and that was something Clay wasn't going to let happen to the man he loved.

"Tate, I'm out the door now." He left the house and moved swiftly to his parked car. "I'll be there soon. Hold on for me, okay?"

When Tate spoke again, his plea broke Clay's heart. He'd never tried to start his car so fast in all his life. His man sounded so damned lost.

"I need you. Please hurry." The line went dead.

Clay thought he'd broken the land speed record by the time he reached the police station and struggled to find somewhere to plant his car. Growling at the lack of parking, he eventually parked on a yellow line and decided any traffic warden giving him a ticket would get a long fuck-you letter if they ticketed him.

He tore into the police station as if all the demons in *Supernatural* were on his tail. The duty officer behind the desk stared at him in surprise as Clay leaned over the desk and barked out, "My partner is here. Tate Williams. Where is he?"

The duty officer blinked. "Sir, I have no idea where he might be I've just got on shift. What was he admitted for?"

"I haven't got a fucking clue," Clay said, panic overriding good manners. "He just called me and told me to come down here. It was something about a young girl dying?"

The officer's face still looked puzzled. "Let me find out for you. Hold on."

He reappeared about five minutes later as Clay tapped his fingers impatiently on the counter. "He's in one of the interrogation rooms, sir, with Sergeant Fisher. He's being questioned."

"Questioned? What the hell for? Has he got a lawyer?" Clay snarled. If it was the same Fisher he knew of, the man had been one of Tate's partners in the past. He was a big, burly, bearded man with a good heart.

The duty officer rolled his eyes. "Tate doesn't need a lawyer. As far as I know he's not accused of anything. He was simply the witness who found the body."

A sliver of cold ran down Clay's spine. "He found a kid's body?" Inside he raged at the unfairness of it all.

Christ, how much more does he have to go through? Wasn't having him tortured and shot and his mind fucked up enough for you, God? Now you have to throw a dead kid at him too? Well, fuck you.

"Please take me to him." Clay demanded.

"He's being moved to the waiting room and you can see him there." The duty officer smiled sympathetically at Clay. "We all know Tate here. He's been through hell in the past and we didn't want to cause him any more trouble. He's in a bit of a mess at the moment though. I think he'll be glad to see a friendly face."

Feeling rather a heel at his high-brow attitude, Clay tried to smile. "Thank you. I'm sorry if I seem a little agitated, but you know…" He shrugged and took a deep breath. "He's special to me." He had no idea whether his and Tate's relationship was common knowledge yet, so he thought it best to play it quiet. Tate had enough on his plate.

The policeman grinned. "No need to be circumspect, Mister Mortimer. We know you two are *together*-together. Tate's nephew Rick is a frequent visitor here."

"Ah. I see." Clay wasn't sure he liked the fact that Rick had been the Gay Town Crier about his and Tate's relationship but the damage was done. "Thanks." He looked around. "Can I see him now then?"

The other man nodded. "Sure. Follow me."

His portly frame led the way to a colourless, soulless room in which slumped a man who had definitely seen better days. Tate's face was drawn and pale, his eyes dark circles in his face. He was wearing unfamiliar clothing—an old Iron Maiden tee shirt and what looked like a ratty pair of long grey joggers. He sat looking down at his hands twisting around and around in some frenzied parody of hand washing. Clay's heart ached to see him looking so vulnerable and beaten.

"Tate?" he murmured quietly. Tate looked up, eyes widening, and then stood up, only to launch himself into Clay's open arms. Clay pulled him close, feeling Tate's body shivering as he wrapped his warm arms around him with the fierce determination never to let him go again.

"Christ, it's good to see you." Tate's muffled words against his sweatshirt had Clay swallowing down his emotions.

"I'll leave you two alone then," said the duty officer, who turned and left the waiting room.

Clay held Tate to him, feeling his heartbeat through the fabric of his clothing.

"Not sure I like your fashion choice," he murmured, breathing in Tate's smell. "You look like the remnant of someone out of a drug dive search."

Tate's hands tightened on Clay's hips. "I had to give them my other clothes. They were covered in blood."

Clay shuddered. "God, love, what the hell happened?"

Tate told him. Everything.

Five minutes later, his heart cracking open with pain and empathy, Clay sat as he watched his lover fall apart. All he could do was stand there and hug the man crying silently against his chest in his arms and promise him things would be okay.

****

Three days after the incident, Clay sat and watched Tate sitting on the couch, freshly showered, in his own comfortable clothes and staring unseeingly at the television. Lately he'd eaten listlessly, but tonight Clay had managed to get some pasta down him. Tate had a glass of neat whisky next to him, which had been hardly touched.

The inroads they'd made on Tate's nightmares had been dented by this latest tragedy but Tate was still coping better than Clay though he would. His lover did sometimes wake up with a start with all the monsters in his head and all Clay could do was hold him or sometimes make love to him, until Tate settled back into an uneasy and restless sleep.

The one thing he wasn't prepared to let Tate do was feel guilty for the situation he'd been forced into once again. Guilt was something Tate had in abundance in his over-packed suitcase of emotions, along with self-recrimination and shame. Any more shoved in there and the suitcase would burst open, showering them all with the acrid aftermath of the explosion.

Clay sat down beside Tate and pulled him against Clay's side. With a soft sigh, his boyfriend leaned against him, and his hand ran across Clay's stomach, seeking the warmth and solace of his skin under the open shirt he wore. Clay's hand moved up to gently stroke the bristles of Tate's hair, bristles that were longer than normal and which Clay thought suited him.

"I'm going to say something to you and I don't want you to go off pop," he murmured against Tate's hair.

Tate huffed. "*That's* a helluva positive conversation starter," he muttered and closed his eyes as Clay massaged his scalp with strong fingers. A faint, pleased growl of satisfaction from Tate made Clay smile. The big, bad, tough undercover cop had a secret weakness when it came to this particular action. He turned into a great big puppy.

Clay tried to find the right words. "It's been a few days now so I think I can say them. Whatever you'd have done differently the other night—don't let it take you over. Don't second guess yourself and think *if only*. That's not going to help anyone. This whole thing wasn't your fault. I know you will, but I don't want it to consume you. You've suffered enough, love. You still suffer."

He kept massaging Tate's scalp as he waited for the reply. Finally it came. It was a soft murmur of assent that made Clay's heart beat faster.

"I know, and you're right. I did some thinking of my own." He gave a strained chuckle. "And at the station the other day Clem laid into me too about how narcissistic I was being if I thought I could cure the world's ills or stop people killing themselves." He sighed. "I guess the old adage about 'there's always someone out there worse off than you' is true after all."

Tate valued his ex-partner and Clay was glad the man had spoken to him. Tate's sister, Lucy, who was now aware of their relationship and happy about it, had also come by to talk sense into her brother.

"I'm glad you listened to him and Lucy." Clay pressed a soft kiss to Tate's head.

Tate sighed. "Yet you tell me the same thing and to quote your words, 'I go off pop.' Why does it always make more sense when you hear stuff from other people?"

Clay snorted. "It's like kids. You tell your child to get off the furniture and they don't listen. But let someone else tells them and the chances are that they'll listen."

Tate sat up and stared at him with narrowed eyes. "You're calling me a child?" He reached over and palmed Clay's groin suggestively. "Would a child do that to you?"

Clay grinned, pleased to see his old Tate coming back. "I'd fucking hope not. That would be wrong. But a sexy man with eyes like yours and a mouth that looks like it needs shutting up with mine—that I wouldn't mind."

He was growing harder at Tate's slow brushes against his cock, and from the look in his eyes that was exactly what his lover wanted. In his head Clay chuckled.

Tate using sex as comfort. I'll never complain about that. As long as it makes him forget things for a while.

He grinned as his pants were unzipped and Tate's tongue came out to wet his very kissable lips. At that sight, Clay's cock instantly plumped up. The sly caress of Tate's thumb across the head of his dick made it even perkier. Clay settled comfortably back against the couch, stretching his arms across the back, hitching a breath as Tate's mouth swallowed him down. The image of Tate's mouth on him, dark head bobbing up and down with his little moans of pleasure teasing his cock, never failed to arouse Clay. Tate was exceptionally good at sucking cock and enjoyed it immensely. His hot, wet tongue flicking against Clay's tip, those long, steady licks against his shaft as Tate glanced up at Clay, holding him mesmerised. The fact this was *his* Tate was a turn-on itself.

"Your mouth is too good at this," Clay hissed, eyes closing in bliss as Tate took him deep, throat massaging his sensitive dick. "I know I say that every time." His voice caught as Tate's tongue did something to him that sent all the nerve endings in his body aflame. "Christ that felt good. Do it again."

Tate's gave a wicked chuckle as his dirty mouth drove Clay crazy. When he pulled off, Clay moaned pitifully.

"Don't bloody stop," he groaned huskily. "Finish me off, please, in your mouth."

Tate shook his head. "No. You need to get those jeans off," he growled. "I'm going to fuck you this time. Make you come when I'm inside you."

Clay needed no prompting. He shifted his hips, lifted his arse and had his jeans and briefs off in record time. He left his shirt on. Tate liked it when he was half dressed. His lover wasted no time unbuttoning his own jeans, and as he pushed his black briefs down, his cock sprung out. Clay's backside throbbed in anticipation of having it inside him.

"You want to move this to the bedroom?" he murmured as he watched Tate run a hand up and down his erection, eyes dark and needy.

"Nope. Going to do it right here, on the couch. Get on your knees and hold on. I'm coming in for landing."

Clay laughed softly as he switched around to kneel on the couch, arse stuck out in the air, hands gripping the arm. "Don't forget the oil, Maverick," he breathed as Tate's fingers slid over the curve of his backside. "It's been a little while."

Tate sniggered as he reached under one of the throw cushions and found the lube. There was always a tube handy in the Mortimer household. Clay thought he might have been a Boy Scout in a previous life.

"Don't worry. I'll make sure you're all oiled up before I fly you."

Clay gave a snort of laughter. "Where the hell are all these aviation references coming from anyway? Have you been reading those bloody Dale Brown books again…? Oh hell, Tate. Yes…"

Tate had crawled on the couch behind him and the cold slickness of lube with its minty fragrance being rubbed against his hole made Clay lose his train of thought. His cheeks were spread open, and insistent fingers circled his opening and then slipped inside, opening him up. Talented fingers pushed their way in to stroke Clay's prostate and the zings of pleasure made his skin prickle and his arse clench tightly around Tate's welcome intrusion.

Soft kisses peppered his back, as Tate leaned over him and trailed his tongue down the skin that was already goose bumped with needy sensations. His lover's warm skin pressed against Clay's own heated flesh and a quick bite to his shoulder made Clay's cock jerk. He moaned softly and heard Tate's quiet laugh.

"You taste so damn good. Ready for take-off, Captain?" His cock nudged Clay's hole and Clay nodded, as he took a deep breath.

"God, yes, I need you inside me, to feel you. Stop the damned flight deck talk and just fuck me, please."

Tate sputtered with laughter as he pushed inside Clay. "I like talking dirty flight talk. Oh God, yes…" He gave a hiss of satisfaction as he slid deep inside, filling Clay with his heat and hardness. Clay pushed back against Tate's groin.

"You can do better than that," he gasped as he closed his eyes and concentrated on the heady feeling of Tate inside him. "Come on, where's my big, bad hard arse of a cop? I want him. I need him to show me just what a bastard he can be."

Tate gave a low, dangerous snarl and began pounding Clay in earnest, the denim of his half-mast jeans rubbing against Clay's skin. When Tate had been in the force, one of the things they'd done had been role play. In the early days, fucking each other while Tate had his old police uniform on had been something they'd both enjoyed. The handcuffs still came into play and were enjoyable, but Tate in his uniform, shirt unbuttoned, pants open and that cock of his rising from the depth of the formal trousers had been a sight for sore eyes.

Clay closed his eyes and surrendered to the power and passion of the man behind him, the grunts and heavy breaths and occasional expletives music to his ears. He revelled in Tate's scent, his presence and his sweating skin and heated flesh. Clay's own rising emotions and awareness of just how much he loved the man inside him filled his heart, just as Tate filled him.

He grunted when Tate's hand came around and fastened around his cock, jerking him off in rhythm with his thrusts, inflaming Clay's senses and bringing him to the brink.

"Just like that," he panted, "Don't stop. Make me come."

Tate's nip of Clay's ear nearly drove him over the edge. "Oh I intend to," Tate hissed. "I love to feel you come around my cock. Love it when you tighten on me, pulse like a fucking strobe light. I can lose myself when you come like that, Clay."

His thrusts grew deeper, fiercer and his teeth closed on the tender flesh on the side of Clay's shoulder.

This fucking hurts but I love it...

With a strained cry, Clay felt his balls contract, felt his groin tighten and the familiar wash of sexual gratification as it soaked his body and ushered in his climax. Arcs of his release jetted across the couch, flooding Tate's hand and Clay's belly with sticky fluid. His body tensed and then slackened, and his arms threatened to give way on the arms of the couch with the intensity of his orgasm. It was made worse as Tate rammed harder into Clay, causing him to almost fall over the chair arm. With a soft snort, Clay braced himself for his lover's last final pushes into his now tender hole.

When Tate topped, Clay always knew when he came. He made a hoarse, throaty grunt and gripped Clay tightly, fingers digging into his flesh and leaving marks. He was a biter too, as evidenced by the teeth marks on Clay's body and the nips to his ears. Tate's groin was all but melded to Clay's backside, as if he was trying to fuse with him, as his cock throbbed while he shot copious amounts of come inside Clay. Clay loved the feel of it inside him, marking him.

Tate lay across Clay's back, breath warm in his ear. "That was fucking awesome," he panted. "It's been some time since I had you like that."

Clay made a face. His arms were tired from supporting himself and his partner's weight. Thank God he worked out. "Yeah, except you nearly made me fall arse over face on the bloody floor," he laughed softly. "I thought you were trying to launch a rocket up there. Lose yourself in me."

Tate moved out of him and off him, leaving Clay to push himself up and try not to get the come from his arse all over the couch as well as everything else.

"I always lose myself when I'm with you," Tate murmured, his lips curving in a warm smile. "It's where I belong." He hitched his jeans and stained underwear up. "I'm going to shower. You can join me if you like, and I'll wash you down."

Clay stood up and bent down to pick up his trousers off the floor. "I'll be there in a minute. Get it hot for me." He snorted at Tate's cheeky grin. "Not that, you fool, although if you think you can get it up again…" He shrugged as Tate cackled.

"I'm the younger one in this relationship," Tate teased. "I should be saying that to you." He evaded Clay's fist aimed at his arm and escaped into the hallway.

Clay shook his head as he used his underwear to clean up the mess they'd left on his expensive fabric couch. Thank God for Scotchgard, he thought with a wry grin. It was probably time to get the cleaners in again though and have another dose of it applied. Couch- fucking looked as if it could become a regular occurrence.

Chapter 10

The smell woke Tate up. It pervaded his nostrils with its stink and left a sour metallic taste in his mouth. He opened his eyes in disgust and panic, hands fumbling in front of his face as if trying to push someone away. He took a deep breath, imagining the lingering essence of blood on his tongue. In the darkness of the room Clay slept on, and Tate was glad he hadn't shouted out this time and woken up his lover. He shivered in the aftermath of his nightmare and sighed tiredly.

I am so damn tired of this shit.

Tate had once again been dreaming about Lily—and Armerian. In the dream, he'd seen the young girl lying there still and cold, the blood pooling about her body. Tate lay next to her, drenched in blood, cold, shivering and hurting. In the shadows, a man lurked, invisible but Tate knew it was his dead tormentor. Deep in the pools of his mind, the deep, dark lakes of his psyche, Sonny Armerian always lurked, like a silent, grinning predator ready to eat his flesh.

At times like this Tate wished he smoked so he could light up a cigarette and sit by the window, staring out in the darkness beyond it, blowing plumes of smoke and focusing on it as it swirled in the still air. It always looked so cool in the movies.

He shivered, remembering the weariness in Lily's young voice and the look of defeat on her face. The fact he'd not pushed her into accepting his help would always rankle with him. But he'd acknowledged, despite what everyone might have thought about him trying to blame himself, he was *not* to blame. He'd been spending more time at Castaways, trying to make sure he made a difference to kids who needed him. Trying to show them that people could be trusted and not everyone was an abuser. Jax was especially a delight for Tate. The young man was funny, occasionally moody, intelligent and one of the warmest and empathic people that Tate knew. He was like a little brother and that was something Tate could get on board with.

He sat up, leaning over to pick up his mobile on the nightstand. He flicked through the picture gallery and came to the picture he'd always carry around.

The photo of the note Lily had left him.

The police had taken the original but Tate had taken a picture of it with his mobile before it had disappeared. He wanted something to remember her by other than the dreams he had.

"Can't you sleep?" Clay's husky tones caused Tate to turn and look at him. His partner's eyes were sleepy, and his face furrowed with sleep lines.

Tate smiled softly at him. "I had a bit of a bad dream. I'm fine. Go back to sleep."

Clay yawned and stretched, the covers slipping down until Tate could see the firm planes of his stomach and the treasure trail of dark hair that led down to his sleep shorts. It was a sight he'd never grow tired of.

"I'm awake now, and it's"—Clay squinted at the wrist watch he never removed—"five a.m. anyway. So, the middle of the morning, really."

Tate snorted. "For a soldier like you, maybe, Mister SAS. For those others of us a little more refined, it's fuck o'clock."

Clay's face lit up. "Really? Is that an actual time then? Because I like the sound of that time of day." He chuckled as Tate huffed in exasperation. "You walked right into that one, babe." His face grew serious. "So what woke you?"

Tate sighed and leaned against the headboard, hands clasped behind his head. He hated that Clay had to ask that question. "Just memories."

Clay shifted in the bed, getting comfortable. "I wish I could take it all away for you. It pisses me off I can't reach inside that head of yours and pluck it all out."

Tate sighed heavily. "Me too." He managed a wry grin. "We'd be millionaires if we could." His hand moved up idly to touch the scar on his chest. "This was bad enough but then the thing with Lily…it's just not fair, you know? She was so damn young."

Clay nodded. "When kids die, there's something about it…" his voice trailed off and Tate knew he was remembering something from his past. Clay's jaw clenched; the tic in his cheek became more prominent when he was emotional.

"Tell me about it, please," Tate murmured, moving to his side and propping himself up on his elbow. He fixed his eyes on Clay's face. "How do you get over it?"

Clay's eyes shadowed. "You don't. It's always there with you. But the memory gets less painful as time goes on. That's what I've found and what I keep trying to tell *you*." He smiled to take the sting out of his words. He looked as if he was considering his words carefully. "I was with a group in Israel about eight years ago. We went over to do recon on some Palestinian activity, some rebels who were operating in a camp out in the desert. It was all ultra-secret, of course, one of those field ops where plausible deniability was the buzz word." He snorted in derision. "Bastards who sit behind a desk, and who've never seen blood close up in all their damn lives, telling us that if we fuck up no one's coming to fetch us. We were on our own."

Tate nodded in fascination. He'd heard many tales of Clay's past, but only the ones that could be told. Clay had a lot of stories that Tate suspected remained hidden away in the recesses of his sharp, agile mind, never to be shared—never to be forgotten.

"There were a number of young boys among the rebel camp. Three of them, aged between about ten and twelve. They carried guns, looked too young to be there in such a damn inhospitable terrain. It was blistering hot; the sand flies bit any open flesh they could find and even found their way up your butt crack." He smiled slightly as Tate made a noise of disgust. "I found smearing Vaseline around my hole and between my cheeks at least protected me from the bites and made sure they didn't crawl up my arse."

Tate's backside clenched in sympathy. "That sounds like a fate worse than death," he murmured, running his hands over Clay's furred chest.

Clay nodded. "Not pleasant." He turned and plumped up his pillows, punching them to make them fluffier then sat back with a satisfied sigh. "We staked out the place for a while, checking what was going on, taking photos and relaying information back to base. It was rumoured that there was an Israeli reporter who'd been captured and was being held. Our brief was if he was there, to extract him and get out. It turned out to be a crock of shit. There was no damn reporter. We were told to get out of there, as they were planning an air attack and hadn't wanted the reporter getting blown to smithereens if they could help it. He apparently had some big wig political father back in Jerusalem." He huffed. "It would have been bad form having his son smeared all over the damn desert."

His eyes grew distant. "As we were sneaking out, one of the kids found us. My point guy hadn't seen him leave the encampment and we came face to face with him with his dick out, taking a piss." Clay's body stilled. "We had decision to make. We couldn't afford him crying out to warn the others, which is what he would have done. It would have jeopardised the air strike."

Clay's face darkened and Tate swallowed. He hoped this wasn't headed where he thought. "What did you do?" he asked quietly.

Clay exhaled loudly. "None of the group wanted to kill a kid. In an ideal situation, with a man or woman, we would have done it there and then. I'm both ashamed and relieved to say we all hesitated. Not good when you've been trained for that eventuality." There was a poignant silence. "Then one of the older rebels came across us and screamed at the kid to shoot us. The look in that kid's eyes…" Clay's voice trailed off. "He couldn't do it. So the guy raised his weapon at the kid and shot him point blank in the head. It was like a fucking melon exploding. The bastard was entertained by it all, and it probably saved our lives."

Tate groaned in horror.

"We had to get out of there pronto before the rest of them came running. I was nearest. While the sick SOB was gloating, I jumped in, snapped the bastard's neck, watched him fall to the ground and yelled to my men to get the hell out of there. Our transport wasn't far so we made it." His voice was matter of fact but Tate heard the pain in it.

"Jesus," Tate had a sick feeling in his stomach at what Clay must have felt. He sat up straight. "You've never told me that story before."

Clay shrugged. "Not one of the highlights of my career, seeing a kid killed like that," he said quietly. "Plus we ignored our training. We could have all gotten killed and stuffed the mission up by getting caught because we couldn't shoot a kid pointing a weapon at us."

Tate swallowed. "That's admirable to me, not something to be ashamed of. You make me feel so damn stupid, like a coward," he whispered.

His lover frowned as he sat up, covers pooling at his waist. "Why would you say that? You're no damn coward." His fierce tone warmed Tate's heart but still he felt a sense of failure.

"Because you have things in your past that could drive you crazy," Tate explained. "You've killed people, been shot at, been in war zones and seen horrible things but you don't have nightmares like I do. You've seen things I probably couldn't even imagine, but you're so damn strong, you can put them to rest. Me?" He sneered. "I fall apart at firecrackers, have bad dreams about kids who've killed themselves, agonise over what happened to me with Armerian when you've probably seen much worse. How do you stay so strong?" He heard the agitation in his voice. "Am I just a fucking wuss that I'm like I am? All damaged?" He threw himself back against the bed, breathing heavily and throwing his arm over his eyes. The sense of emasculation, the feeling he was a weakling tasted like acid in his mouth. He huffed loudly, opening his eyes as a strong, warm weight landed on top of him and his arms were yanked off his shamed face and held above his head.

Clay was aflame with passion, his eyes bright green glints in a tanned face. He looked like a man about to take on the world. "Don't *ever* talk about yourself that way again," he snarled, as his body held Tate's still. Tate gulped at the vehemence in his lover's voice. "You are one of the strongest men I know. What was done to you by that fucking bastard was something you wouldn't have done to an animal. I saw you afterwards, love." His voice cracked with pain. "I saw you shot three times and left to die like a dog on the sidewalk. I saw what he'd done to you. The horrors he'd inflicted."

Tate wanted to close his eyes and not remember but his eyes were hypnotised by Clay's. They stared into him and Tate swore he could see into Clay's soul. He'd never stopped to consider what Clay might have gone through when Tate had been hurt.

"The knife cuts, all the broken bones, the burns. The damage to your balls and cock where he'd kicked you. The brand he carved into your backside as if you were some sort of animal that he fucking owned. The coke up your nose." Clay's voice quietened. "The bites and teeth marks everywhere and the bruising and finger marks around your backside."

Now Tate struggled, the memories of what he'd called 'that which will never be spoken of' rising to the fore like some giant, monstrous leviathan. His shame and his guilt at what he'd done for 'the mission.'

"No, fuck you," he snarled. "We don't talk about that, you bastard." He flailed his arms and Clay pinned him tightly.

"That's the problem," he murmured softly. "You hide it away from me, and deep down, you need to let it out. I think we've both waited long enough." His hands gripped Tate's wrists like a vise. His body shifted on top of Tate's, its warmth and strength both comforting and scary.

"Let me go, Clay." Tate's vision blurred as tears threatened to fall. "I won't talk about that to you." Dr Jakes knew about Tate's deception with Sonny Armerian and his rape at his hands but he'd never told her everything about the sexual savagery that Sonny had inflicted upon him during his torture ordeal. He knew she suspected there was more than he'd told her.

"It's time." Clay's gentle voice was closer now, his lips brushing Tate's cheek.

Tate shook his head stubbornly. "No," he spat at him, still trying futilely to get free. But fighting against someone like Clay, single minded, tough, protective and physically strong, wasn't an option. The man was a fierce warrior, a man used to getting his own way.

"If you love me, Tate, and want us to get through this, you need to tell me." Clay's commanding voice overrode Tate's, which was telling him to hide, keep a secret. He cried out in anger and distress, the tears seeping from his eyes now, bringing back the memories of what Armerian had done to him in those four days. He hadn't only taken his freedom away but his self-respect too. How could any man raped by another not feel that way?

Clay gripped his face and stared into Tate's face with haunted eyes. "What he did to you was not your fault. You were tied up, chained, with no say in what happened. And when you admit that, maybe, just maybe, the nightmares might go away."

Tate was tired. He stopped struggling and simply listened to Clay's voice, hearing the love and grief in it for him.

Maybe it is time to tell him everything. I'm so tired of keeping it a dirty secret. No one else knows what my relationship with Sonny actually was and the guilt is tearing me apart. Clay deserves to know too.

"I was with you when they brought you into the hospital, virtually dead." The dead tone of Clay's voice reached out to Tate. "You flat-lined once, and when they brought you back, I cried like a fucking baby." His voice choked. "We were just friends then but I knew, just knew, that if you got through it I was going to make you mine. No more of this best friend shit. I was going to have you, body and soul. I love you so damn much. I've loved you forever."

"You don't know what I did, Clay." Tate heard his voice but it didn't sound like him. It sounded like a man with everything to lose. "What I did for that damn case. How hard I fell to get what I wanted—to put him away."

What he did to me.

Clay's voice was steady. "Then tell me. Right here, right now. Tell me what you did. What causes you to wake up at night."

He loosened his grip on Tate's wrists and his weight lifted as he rolled to the side. Clay didn't let go of him though; he kept his arm across Tate's chest as he cradled his back.

"I can't," Tate whispered in agony. "You'd see me differently and I never want that to happen."

"Listen to me." Clay's voice was steely. "Nothing you can ever say to me will make me love or respect you less. You are it for me, baby. Everything I want is here." He stroked his fingers down Tate's flanks and his touch grounded Tate. "You need to tell me what went down or you will never fucking heal."

The only sound was both of them breathing and the clamour of Tate's rapidly thudding heart in his aching chest. He was surprised Clay couldn't hear it.

Maybe it's time to admit what I did. What I really was. A whore.

Tate's cheeks were wet. He took a deep breath, then started speaking, his emotions suppressed. "I was told to meet Sonny, get friendly with him."

He heard Clay's indrawn breath at the mention of the man's first name. They'd always called him Armerian in the past, as if there was no personal connection. "We met at the gym he dumped me at when he threw me out the car that night. I took one look and figured it wasn't a hardship trying to get to know him. He was sexy as fuck. Tall, dark-skinned, swarthy, built like a damn powerhouse."

There was another hiss of breath from Clay and his fingers tightened on Tate's hips momentarily before once again stroking his skin. Tate had a sinking feeling Clay knew where this was going. "Yeah, he was a major drug dealer, but hey, that's what it made fun. Knowing what I was there to do, that I was going to bring him down." Tate took a deep breath. This was the hard part. "So I got to know him very well indeed." He stopped and so did the Clay's hand.

"You two were fucking *before* all the shit went down?" The incredulity in Clay's tone made Tate feel dirty and unclean and he wanted to lie. But he'd come this far. He couldn't back out now.

"Yes," he said quietly. "Of course, no one knew. It was bad street cred to have a bisexual head honcho as the kingpin of a drug cartel like Reino. And I never told anyone on the force or in the team we'd become lovers. They just believed I was acting as one of the gang."

Clay released him and sat up, his eyes wide and blew air out of puffed up cheeks. His face was pale. "I knew he was bisexual. It came out in my investigation. He was married to a woman after all. But the two of you together? That's news to me."

Clay stared at Tate with eyes that looked as if he didn't know him at all. It cut Tate to the core. Tate took a deep breath and laid a hand on Clay's arm. Clay stiffened and Tate's throat closed up.

God, he hates me.

"Just, leave me a minute, will you?" Clay's voice was choked. "I need a moment to deal with this."

Despair wrenched at Tate's heart and dealt it a heavy blow. He knew Clay well enough to know that his admission was hurting him. The fact Tate had been fucking a man while he and Clay had been friends and trying to deny whatever was between them for the sake of that friendship *had* to wound Clay deeply. He needed to explain more, see if he could fix this.

Tate sat up, taking a sip from his water glass. "It was for the job," he said softly. "It was the best way to keep him close, get him to trust me." He fiddled with the sheet over his groin, pulling it into folds nervously. He cleared his throat. "I had to do coke now and then just to make sure he trusted me. Other stuff as well, but never anything heavy. I'd seen guys get into the like of H and that shit and there was no way I'd do that, not even for the job." He gave a short bark. "Prostituting myself—I guessed that was okay."

Clay's brows furrowed and he glanced away to look at the wall, eyes distant.

Tate felt the old shame leaking back into his mind. "There was no emotional connection though, at least on my side. It was just sex. Or so I thought." There'd been other things they'd done together—

bondage games and other kinky shit—but Tate would never tell Clay about that part of his relationship with Sonny Armerian. That he definitely *would* take to his grave.

Tate stared at Clay, trying to will him to look at him. Perhaps if he could see Clay's face, he'd know what was coming next. Tate didn't like surprises.

"He obviously kept it discreet and made it known if I ever outed him I'd be a dead man. I don't think I was the first, and while I was undercover, I learnt a bit about other guys he'd had before me who had 'disappeared.' Some of them must have tried blackmail, or maybe he simply he got bored of them and couldn't take any chances." Tate shrugged. "Not many people in his crew knew about his other sexual preferences and those who did were fiercely loyal. I managed to keep his interest until the day he got the phone call in his office telling him about me. We still don't know who leaked it or how it happened." He shrugged. "I doubt we ever will." He cleared his throat. The memories of Sonny's flat eyes looking at him over the top of his John Lennon glasses, the ones he'd worn when he needed to read, still chilled Tate to his core.

"I could see what was going down. I knew I needed to get out of there fast or I'd end up dead. The problem was the door was locked because just minutes before, he'd fucked me on the desk."

Clay finally looked at Tate. His jaw was tight, the tic in his cheek throbbing. Tate knew he had to finish this story. It was as if the dam had burst and the floodtide of self-recrimination and guilt had come rushing out like oily, tainted sludge and was soaking them both with its stench.

"He took his gun out of his desk drawer halfway through the conversation and laid it on the desk. I knew something was wrong then. My gun was still in my holster, on the floor with my pants. I couldn't get to it. He pistol-whipped me across the head before I could even do anything, and then kicked me senseless. When I woke up, I was in a garage, just me and a whole bunch of fancy cars. I knew then it would be a miracle if I got out alive."

Tate's voice was hoarse from talking. He took another gulp of water. His hands were shaking.

What the hell does he think of me? Should I have kept quiet? No, he'd never let it go. This is Clay. He'd have dragged it out of me sometime, might as well be now.

Clay finally spoke, his voice tight. He still didn't look at Tate but kept his gaze centred on the sheets at his waist. "Did you not have any backup to support you? Someone who'd know where you were, and that you hadn't called in? Isn't that standard operating procedure for an undercover op like yours?"

Tate nodded. "There was backup, of course. I couldn't wear a wire of any sort. Too dangerous and in any case, he'd have found it."

Especially with the regularity I had my clothes off.

From the look on Clay's face, he'd had the same thought. Tate wanted to crawl into a dark tunnel and hide.

"So I had a throwaway phone stash, a number to call and told to check in twice a day, using code words—all that shit." He shifted uncomfortably. "But the house we were in was one of his safe houses, and it was a new one. When I finally realised where we were, and that my team didn't know about it, I needed to get away and tell them." His face burned. "Sonny was feeling rather amorous and he jumped me before I could do that. So I thought I'd have time to do it afterwards. Then the call came in and everything went tits up."

"Christ, it sounds like a damn cluster fuck." Clay sounded as if he was trying to hold some emotion back and Tate just hoped it wasn't disgust. He couldn't bear if Clay lost respect for him after this. Their relationship was worth shit without it. He kept quiet, heart aching, the fluttering in his stomach making him nauseous.

"And that's when he decided to torture you?" Clay's tone was soft but dangerous. Tate had no doubt it would strike fear into someone else; shit, he was already scared at the possibility he was going to lose him.

"Yes. He made it a 'project' to do whatever he could to get me to spill the beans about the operation, whether there was anyone else undercover. I kept telling him I was the only one, that there was no one else. I told him I'd never tell him anything about the operation so he might as well kill me now." Tate's eyes burned, and they were gritty with fatigue. "He said he believed me. And that he knew I'd never tell him anything of value no matter what he did. He knew I'd die before that happened."

Clay's nostrils flared. "He believed you, but he carried on. To pay you back for what you'd done to him as opposed to needing information?" He looked up at Tate now, his eyes burning with a violent darkness that Tate had never seen before.

Tate exhaled. "Yes. And yes. The rough sex, rape, whatever you'd call it happened and the rest—" He broke off. There was no way he was telling Clay about what had been done to him with bottles and other household implements during his incarceration. "—that was to punish me too. For leading him on, making him feel something for me. He told me he'd been starting to fall in love with me."

Clay's face was white. "The word rape is the right one." His face was pained as he reached up to touch Tate's jaw softly. Tate wanted to rejoice at the fact his lover was touching him. "And an animal like him didn't know the meaning of the word love. He was a man who thought he could own people. Use them." He frowned. "What did you mean 'the rest'?"

Tate ignored that question. "I was pretty drugged up and in pain. I couldn't do much to fight him off. That first day, after he'd smacked me unconscious, I woke up to him beating me with a golf club. One of his fancy ones he was fond of. He broke my ribs, my arm, and cracked my tibia. He kicked the fuck out of me and then pushed coke up my nose until I was so high I couldn't think." He shuddered and Clay reached out again, laying a hand on Tate's arm, stroking his skin gently.

Tate's eyes prickled with tears at that gesture. "He'd release me, untie me, but I was pretty broken. I wasn't given food or water regularly so I didn't have the strength to fight him off. I tried; believe me. But he broke my nose and collarbone and beat the shit out of me and still took what he wanted anyway. He said it was his right. That I was his."

His voice cracked. He was exhausted and wanted to shut down, curl up in a ball and hibernate. His soul was bruised black and at that moment, he wanted to howl with pain and grief. Memories of the worst time of his life welled up like acid waste. All he wanted to do was hold onto the man who stared at him with eyes that saw into his soul and never let him go.

"God, Clay," Tate whispered brokenly. "Please tell me you still love me. That I haven't fucked this up for good by what I did. By what happened." It was then that his tears fell, hot, burning rivers of shame and guilt. He crumpled the bed sheets in trembling hands, unable to look up at his lover.

Clay gave a shuddering sigh. He sat up, pulling Tate into his arms to lie against his chest, stroking his hair with one hand while the other wiped tears off Tate's cheek.

"Jesus, Tate. You went through hell. Of course I still love you, you stupid bastard. I'll *never* stop loving you."

Clay's arms tightened possessively around Tate as his hands stroked Tate's back. His chest ached with relief at simply being there, at still being loved, and he couldn't stop more sobs escaping from him.

"God." Clay sounded choked up. "I can't believe you've kept all this inside you. Why the *fuck* have you never spoken about this to me or anyone?"

Tate wiped tears from his eyes and tried to take control of his crying jag. "Because I pimped myself out. I was sleeping with a man to get information from him. I'd never done that before, but with Sonny…I *wanted* to. I was crazy about you, but didn't think you felt the same way. I didn't want to spoil our friendship. So I thought, fuck it, I'll find someone who does want me. And he was around. And I was ashamed at what he did to me, the fact I couldn't stop him. I felt dirty, used."

Tate cleared his throat, taking deep, shuddering breaths. His nose was stuffy and he needed to blow it. "Then afterwards—we happened—*we* became *us* and I didn't want to sully our relationship with the fact I'd whored myself out for the job and got fucked up for it. It just didn't feel right telling anyone about that part of the deal. And you can be possessive and I thought perhaps you might feel…cheated." He stared wildly around the room, looking for a tissue.

Clay gave a soft growl, his arm tightening around Tate. "I'm a fucking possessive bastard, yes, but no one should hurt you like that. God, you should have told me this sooner. What's done is done, Tate. And you shouldn't be ashamed of anything that happened to you." He stroked Tate's cheek tenderly then leaned over and reached inside his bedside drawer. He passed a packet of tissues spotted with Minions over to Tate, who gave a watery chuckle at the sight of the bright yellow characters.

"Really? *Despicable Me* tissues? What's next—Pooh Bear pyjamas?"

Clay laughed softly and Tate opened the packet and blew his nose loudly then wiped the wetness from his cheeks and eyes.

He relished Clay's arms around him and leaned against his lover's chest, feeling his beating heart as he closed his eyes. The comforting, rhythmic sound soothed him, eased his aching soul and he never wanted to lose that feeling of belonging. Now he knew Clay didn't resent him or what he'd done, he felt lighter than he had in months. The storytelling *had* been cathartic.

"I didn't want you to see me as weak, Clay." Tate whispered. "Or as some sort of slut. It was the only time I ever did that because I believed the end justified the means. And—" he swallowed, "I never thought I could have *you*."

Clay's answer to that was to drink in Tate's lips like a parched man needing water. Tate surrendered gladly to that possession, heart gladdening that he was still wanted. His lips devoured Clay's with a possession of his own. Finally they came up for air. Both men's lips were swollen and wet.

Clay rubbed a finger over Tate's lip and Tate sucked it in, delighting in seeing Clay's eyes blacken as his pupils expanded.

"I'm not going to push you for more, but don't think I didn't notice you evaded my question about 'the rest.' You'll tell me in your own time, and if not, I can live with that," Clay murmured as he watched Tate's mouth suck his finger, his eyes passionate. Tate's cock hardened at that look. "You went through hell and kept this all locked inside you. I don't see you as weak. I'm not happy about what you did. Another man having you that way? It hurts. I won't lie to you. But I can't be jealous of a sadistic, manipulating bastard who hurt you in unimaginable ways. You did what you thought you had to do and I know that feeling well. Following orders, making the mission successful."

He gripped Tate's jaw tightly, forcing him to look at him. "You ask me how I cope with everything. I was trained by one of the best fighting forces in the world. They teach you how to deal, how to compartmentalise and rationalise what you do. I don't say it's easy, just that it's easier to believe in it when you're doing it for a cause. For your country and for the benefit of other people who will live because of what you did." He kissed Tate again fiercely and Tate moaned at Clay staking his claim. He wanted so badly to be taken, possessed by this man.

"We had a choice to perform that service or not. You didn't. You had that taken away from you with Armerian when he tortured you. That doesn't make you weak. You didn't deserve what you got just because you were sleeping with the guy. In battle we often do things we never thought we would."

Clay's eyes smouldered as he brushed a hand over Tate's hardened cock. "I need to show you how I feel. Make love to you again until you come so hard you explode. Show you that sex with someone you love is better than with someone you merely lust over. And make no mistake; you are mine now and no one else's. I'd fight somebody to the death for you."

He didn't wait for Tate's reply, just slid under the covers and sucked the skin of Tate's stomach into his mouth. Tate's back arched as Clay ran a hand over Tate's thigh, then stroked between his legs, finding that sensitive part of him. When Clay's mouth finally found Tate's cock, and that hot, wicked mouth licked and sucked with abandon, Tate had no choice but to forget and surrender.

He cried out loudly as he came into Clay's hot, greedy mouth; and when Clay pinned him down, Tate's body rejoiced in being loved, being cherished by Clay's loving thrusts inside him. Tate's hands never left Clay's skin; his need to hold his man close and absorb him was so desperate he thought he might stop breathing. His arse ached from Clay's passion, his mouth was bruised from Clay's possession and his mind was so in tune with his lover's that they were one.

Make me yours. Possess me.

"You are mine," Clay growled as he jerked inside Tate with the force of his orgasm. "I will always be here for you no matter what."

Tate felt the warmth of Clay's seed inside him, marking him, owning him, and he pressed his face into Clay's neck, finally acknowledging that the truth may just have set him free.

Chapter 11

Two weeks after his emotional confession, on a warm early July afternoon, Tate went back to Castaways. He was feeling positive about it being a great day to give a group of kids a talk on what he'd done as a policeman all those years ago. When he got to Castaways and saw Randy and Jen's harassed faces greeting him at the door, he stepped inside with a frown.

"What's wrong? Are the kids all okay?"

Randy flapped a hand at him, as he shook his head. "Oh no, they're fine. Well, all except one." He pursed his lips. "Our Mister Jackson Grady—Jax—has been pitching a hissy fit. He's locked his bedroom door and refuses to let anyone in."

Tate's heart sank. "What happened? Do you think he'll talk to me?" He'd storm up the stairs if need be and insist Jax talk to him.

Randy's face brightened. "Would you mind? He's quite fond of you. I know the two of you have been in touch. I can't get anything out of him other than the command to fuck off and leave him alone. Jax doesn't swear often so we know it's bad when he does. He's not usually so disrespectful."

Jen touched Tate's arm. "I'll go pop the kettle on," she said softly and left the hallway.

Tate nodded his thanks as he hung his windbreaker on a hook on the wall alongside various coloured cardigans and jerseys belonging to the kids. He grinned when he saw a baseball cap there with the words 'Diesel Rules' emblazoned across the top and a picture of a scowling Vin Diesel on the front. He conjured his own fantasies about the man and tried not to blush. "Who's the Vin fan then? He has good taste."

Jen glanced at the cap and smiled. "Oh that belongs to Krispin. He adores the man. His bedroom is plastered with pictures of him." She shrugged. "He's eleven and Vin is his hero and Krispin thinks Vin would protect the little blighter from his dad." Her tone was sad. "His dad's been in prison for child abuse for quite a few years now so he won't be calling anytime soon, but still Krispin worries."

Tate's throat ached at the story of a child who could need a hero like Krispin did. "I've seen people do bad things, but abusing a kid has to be the worst of the worst." A loud bang from above made them both look up the stairs.

Randy sighed heavily. "That'll be Jax. He tends to throw stuff when he gets upset." His face twisted in a wry grin. "Thank heavens it's not often. That young man has a temper on him."

Tate smiled. "I know the feeling. Let me see if he'll talk to me." He made his way up the stairs to the sight of two wide-eyed kids sitting on the landing, half-eaten sandwiches in hand, staring at a door that Tate presumed was Jax's. It was the little kid who'd made Tate eat liquorice—Damon, no, Damien—with an older child Tate hadn't seen before. They gazed at him curiously.

He lifted his chin in greeting and gestured to the door. "Is that Jax's room?"

Both kids nodded solemnly.

"He's not feeling so good, huh?" Tate crouched down beside the two children and smiled sympathetically. "Anyone know what put the bug up his arse?"

Both kids shook their heads. Damien giggled a bit at Tate's words.

"He just got grumpy and said he was going to his room," the unknown child muttered. "He got a text and it made him mad."

Tate filed that away for future reference. "Do you know who it was on the phone?"

Again there was the shake of two small heads. Damien spoke softly. "Krispin said we should maybe go downstairs and ask Jen if we can bake him a cake to make him feel better. Jax likes chocolate cake and maybe it will make him smile again." His lower lip quivered. "I don't like it when Jax is sad. It makes me sad 'cos he's always so happy."

Tate's heart ached. "That sounds like a really good idea to me," he agreed, looking at the kid he supposed must be Krispin, lover of all things Vin Diesel. "Why don't you go down and ask her and I'll see if I can talk to Jax and find out what's wrong with him?"

Both boys looked doubtfully at each other.

"You can try," said Krispin quietly. "Normally we just leave him alone and he comes down to dinner sometimes." He stood up and took little Damian's hand. "Come on, squirt. Let's go downstairs and see if Jen will let us bake."

He nodded his head at Tate and the two boys made their way down the stairs. Tate took a deep breath and knocked on the door.

"I told you all to fuck off!" An expected reply said vehemently.

Tate sighed. "Yeah, well I've just arrived and I have no intention of leaving just yet. Stop being such a damn drama queen and open the door and let's talk."

There was a silence. Then, "Who the hell are you?"

Tate rolled his eyes. "We've spoken enough on the phone, Jax. You know who it is. It's Tate."

"Just go away. I don't want to talk to anyone." There was a soft muttering from behind the door and Tate grinned. No doubt Jax was asking himself why nobody wanted to listen, to leave him alone. Tate had done it often enough himself.

He sat down on the landing outside Jax's door. "I'm not going anywhere, so I'll just wait here until you open the door. I have a cup of tea on the way and maybe a piece of chocolate cake too. I'm in no hurry." He got comfortable sitting against the wall next to Jax's door and took out his mobile and texted Clay.

Guess what I'm doing? Trying to talk a sulky teenager out of his room.

He closed his eyes as he leaned back and smiled. Clay had done this often enough to him, wheedling, cajoling and finally threatening Tate out of a locked room. Tate knew how this all worked. The key word was patience. His mobile buzzed. He sniggered when he read Clay's message.

Talk about payback. See what it feels like on the other side of the door. Good luck

Jen arrived then with his cup of tea. She snorted and placed it next to him.

"You might have a long wait," she advised. "He's a stubborn little cuss." Her voice rose loudly at the last words, no doubt hoping Jax heard them.

Tate shrugged. "I have time. I'm busy mulling over my speech I was going to give the kids, which has now been delayed." He deliberately spoke louder too. Jen gave him a soft smile and disappeared into one of the bedrooms. Tate shifted, getting comfortable.

There was a scuffling on the other side of the door. "Why are you being such a dick?" the voice asked sulkily.

"It's in my nature." Tate said airily. "My partner accuses me of it all the time, especially when I lock myself in my room and refuse to talk to anyone. Normally his use of the word dick is preceded by another bad word which I won't repeat, because there are small ears around."

There was a soft snort from the other side of the door and Tate's heart lifted. "That's not all he calls me either. His favourite is usually preceded by the bad word and has arsehole after it. So I guess he's an equal opportunity insulter, insulting both my front and my back side."

There was a louder snort now. Tate waited. Then there was the click of a lock turning and Tate stood up, his scarred arse cheek stinging from sitting on it. He tried the door. It swung open and he walked into a darkened room, leaving the door part open behind him.

A huddled shape lay on the bed, duvet cover over his legs and hips, facing away. A dim bedside light was on. The curtains were closed and under the sweet smell of incense, which burned on a side table, the room stank of stale sweat and old deodorant.

Tate's nose twitched. "Quite the aroma café you have going on here. Do you mind if I open a window?"

"Yes."

Tate sighed heavily. "Fine. I'll just asphyxiate with teenage odours."

"I didn't ask you to come in. You bullied your way in here. So put up with the *aromas*."

Tate once again rolled his eyes.

Heaven save me from teenage angst. I think maybe I should have stuck to psychotic drug dealers.

He walked around to the chair by the window, one in front of where Jax lay. He sat down and observed the face of the young man on the bed, lying in what looked like a sweatshirt and jeans. Even in the dim light, he could see the swollen red eyes, the pink nose and the duvet tightly fisted in one pale hand. Jax had been crying and Tate wanted to find out why. He had an overwhelming need to be of solace to this boy curled up in his bed. He was uplifted by the fact that Jax had let him in; it meant he wasn't as averse to being helped as he pretended.

Everybody needs somebody to talk to—even you.

Clay's words echoed in his head and Tate scowled. He wasn't sure he liked being on the other side of the equation. It meant Clay was right.

"Why are you scowling like that?" Jax's voice was thick with crying and from a blocked nose. "You look like you want to punch someone. Is it your partner—your work partner?" His tone was indifferent but Tate heard the underlying curiosity about his use of the word.

"Yes and no. I work for him but he's also my life partner. Clay is my boyfriend."

Jax stilled. The hand clutching the duvet unfurled and Tate heard a slight gasp. He leaned back in the chair and stretched his legs in front of him, and waited.

Finally the bundle of clothes and duvet moved and Jax sat up. His eyes stared at Tate and while Tate couldn't see the expression, his tone indicated surprise—wonder even.

"You're gay?"

"Uh-huh. All my life. Born this way, as Gaga says. Is that a problem?"

"Er, no." Jax stammered. "Of course not. Do I look like a fucking homophobe?" he hissed angrily.

Tate smiled inwardly. Finally, some real emotion.

"Nope. Just wanted to make sure that you weren't one of those 'bad-word' dick arseholes."

There was silence. "Shouldn't it be one of those dicks 'bad-word' arseholes instead?" Jax asked acerbically. He swung his legs over the side of the bed and, head tilted, stared challengingly at Tate who ran the words through his head and grinned when he realised what Jax meant.

"Clever. Not that I'm getting into my sex life with you or anything, but you are a quick one, aren't you?"

Jax's next murmured words would normally have been out of earshot, but Tate's hearing was damned good. He wondered if this was what was bothering Jax.

"Yes, well, that's not anything I'm ever likely to *get into* anyway." Jax crossed his arms over his chest.

Tate leaned forward. "Jax, the kids said you got a text that upset you," he said softly. "Anything you want to talk about? I'm a damn good listener." He felt a pang of guilt suddenly because he hadn't managed to help Lily even though he'd listened to her too. He shoved that thought from his head. He'd been doing okay keeping those emotions at bay and he wanted it stay that way.

Jax's eyes shifted to his mobile on the bedside table. His hands fidgeted in his lap. "Nothing I want to get into."

"Fair enough. So is that the reason you've been a real diva and locked yourself in here? Everyone was worried about you."

Jax shot up so quickly he almost hit Tate on the nose with his flailing arm. He stood and stared down at Tate.

"God, I have one bad period from trying to be so damn happy all the time and everyone gets all bent out of shape about it. Aren't I allowed to be selfish every now and then? To wallow a bit?" His voice shook. "I'm fucking human too, you know, even though people don't think so. They think I'm a freak." He swallowed and Tate saw the sheen of tears in those ruined eyes. His heart ached at the pain etched on Jax's marred face.

"You're not a damn freak," Tate said firmly. "Who the hell's been telling you that nonsense?"

Jax moved over to the window, hugging himself. "Maybe you should go. I'm really not good company right now." His voice broke and what little self-composure he'd been holding onto disappeared as his body shuddered with silent sobs. Tate certainly wasn't going to leave him in this emotional state. He stood up and pulled Jax to him, wrapping him in his arms and patting his back. Jax resisted at first but then heaved a shuddering sigh and leaned into him.

Tate hadn't thought too far ahead on this one. He did think briefly how this would look if anyone walked in and he was found holding Jax this way, but Tate wasn't prepared to let this young man do everything on his own.

"It's fine," he murmured soothingly. "You don't have to tell me everything but I'm here if you want to talk."

Jax sniffed and moved away from Tate, wiping his eyes on the sleeve of his sweatshirt. "Sorry. I didn't mean to do that. I think I got snot on your top."

Tate chuckled. "Don't worry. It won't be the first time. Normally it's my own though."

Jax gave a watery laugh. "Thanks for the image." He walked to his dressing table and fumbled with a tissue box then blew his nose loudly. When he turned around he was more composed.

"You're not a freak." Tate waved a hand. "You're a bright, incredible young man who has his own fan base in this house and who, despite everything he's been through, is strong and independent. And yes, sometimes I think we're all at fault for expecting someone to always be upbeat and not have down days. Of *course* you get to have hippo days."

Jax frowned. "Hippo days?"

Tate grinned. "When you wallow. Like a hippo in mud."

Jax snorted, the corners of his mouth lifting slightly. "Another great image." His face shadowed. "I'm just tired, you know? Of always trying to be Happy Jax. Sometimes I want to scream, tear things up and just feel sorry for myself. The kids…" his voice trailed off. "I love them, and I want to be positive for them but sometimes…" His voice hardened. "Then I get a text from some fucking twat who has no idea who I really am other than what they see outside and it just pisses me off."

Tate didn't *want* to push but he remembered the last time he *hadn't* and how that ended. He wasn't doing it again. "What twat was that?"

For a minute he thought Jax wouldn't answer but then the young man shrugged. "Someone I met whom I thought might be a friend. Or more."

"More? Like a girlfriend?"

Jax hesitated and a shadow flitted across his face. "We met at the library and I really thought maybe I'd found someone who saw past my face to the real me. I was obviously wrong." He gestured to his phone. "I asked the person to coffee and I got a text back saying, sorry, but no thanks. 'Going out of town' was the excuse, without an idea of when they'd be back." He grunted. "I know a brush off when I see one. It's why I don't get friendly with people."

Tate remembered Randy saying Jax had few friends. "So what? Maybe she *is* going out of town. Maybe she'll get hold of you when she gets back."

"And maybe they won't." Jax's tone was bitter. "All I want is someone to be with me, even kiss. Do you know I've never kissed anyone properly? Like with tongue?"

Tate cleared his throat uncomfortably. He was a bit out of his depth in this conversation about French kissing.

Jax gestured to his face. "I kissed someone once before this but it was nothing special. I want a real kiss, maybe more. A *lot* more."

Tate didn't know what to say. Giving sex advice to a teenager was a little out of his comfort zone.

"Maybe you should wait until the right person comes along," he proffered weakly. "They will, Jax. You're no freak, honestly. Someone will see the real you."

Jax shook his head in frustration. "Yeah, right. My face isn't exactly a beacon for hope in that regard and the fact that I'm half blind? I'm a real catch." His voice was scornful. "How do you think it feels to be a seventeen, nearly eighteen-year-old virgin? My hand has never seen so much action."

Tate winced. It wasn't that he was a prude, far from it with his kinks, but this was *so* not a discussion he wanted to have with a seventeen-year-old. "It'll happen, in time. Maybe you need to get out a bit more. I've been told you don't do that much. The odds are more in your favour if you do."

Jax's pale blue eyes stared at him fiercely. "I've resigned myself to the fact that I'll probably die a virgin," he spat. "No one wants damaged goods." He threw himself down onto the bed and wrapped his arms around himself. Tate sat down next to him.

"You're wrong," he said softly. "*I'm* damaged goods, Jax. I went through a really bad time a couple of years ago and nearly died. It left me with a lot of issues." He hitched a breath as he rolled up his sleeves and Jax's eyes widened at the scars on his wrist.

Tate pulled up his shirt, revealing his scarred torso. "Someone did a number on me with a razor blade and a scalpel. He was having fun trying to create a chess board. Then he decided he'd had enough and shot me. But I survived."

Jax's eyes widened in horror as he tilted his head to better see Tate's chest.

Tate shrugged. "I'm still getting over it. Some people aren't so lucky. A couple of weeks ago I was down at the old swimming baths and met this homeless girl called Lily. Thirteen years old. I went away to buy her some food, and when I came back, she was dead. She'd killed herself."

Jax gave another gasp of horror, his hand raised to his mouth.

Tate carried on. "It made me realise something. It made me remember that I *do* have someone, unlike Lily. I have Clay, who loves me, cares enough about me to try and help me fix myself. It took us a long time—over twenty years in fact—to realise we wanted and needed each other and now I'll be damned if I ever let him go. He's my rock." He leaned forward and touched Jax's shoulder gently. "And one day you'll find yours."

Jax stared at him speechlessly. Then his lips twisted in a wry smile. "Wow, this is a real Hallmark moment, isn't it?" His tone wasn't derogatory, more self-deprecating. "I'm sorry, I don't mean to be facetious, Tate. I'm just processing everything you've told me. First you're gay, and then that you've been some through shit yourself. One day maybe you'll tell me all of it. Like why you got those." He waved at the scars.

"One day maybe," Tate agreed. He knew he'd never share all of it but if he could make Jax feel better for the moment, then so be it.

They sat in companionable silence for a few minutes then Jax sighed. "I guess I should shower, clean up my room and get rid of the stench of teenager." He punched Tate lightly on his arm. "Then maybe I'll join you for some of that chocolate cake the kids are baking for me." He gave a wicked smile as he stood up.

Tate chuckled and got up too. "You are too much, young Jax. Clay's going to love you when he meets you."

Jax stared at him uncertainly as he nibbled his bottom lip. "Can I ask you something, and please don't take offence. What's it like—being in a relationship with a man?"

Tate's warning bells rang at that question. "Like any other relationship. Two people getting through the day and doing stuff together. Other than the physical sex bit, there's no difference." His tone grew wry. "Or at least there shouldn't be."

Jax's tongue protruded as he considered his next question. "How did you know?"

"Know what?"

"That you were gay?"

Tate considered. "I think jacking off to *Sports Illustrated* and sucking Billy Grant's dick back in school when I was thirteen was a pretty big indicator." Jax's amused snort warmed his heart. "I'd been eying Billy out for a while and when I got the chance in the showers to try him out, I did." Tate shrugged. "It all made perfect sense. I'd never been interested in girl parts like boobs and stuff." He'd never told Clay about *that* little cock-sucking episode either. Knowing

Clay's jealous streak, the least he knew about Tate's foray into gay man life back in school when they'd been friends the better. "And that, my friend, is between you and me. Clay isn't to know."

Jax sniggered as he picked up clothes from the floor and went to draw the curtains and open a window. "Right, pinkie-swear." He waved at the door. "Now get out and let me get my shit together."

Tate nodded. "On my way." He moved toward the door.

"Tate, wait."

He turned to look at Jax.

"Thanks, for everything." Jax said quietly. "Sometimes a person needs a little perspective, you know?"

Tate grinned. "Better than anyone." He left Jax behind, his body buzzing with energy and a warm glow. He might be a bit of a fuck-up himself, but he seemed to have done someone some good today. His therapy session next week? He was *so* going to impress Dr. Natalie Jakes.

Chapter 12

"So you think you're some sort of psychotherapist now, do you?" Clay teased as he negotiated a bend in the road with expertise. "Like I said before, I bet talking about sex with a seventeen-year-old really made your day." He laughed loudly as Tate gave him the finger.

"I didn't say that," Tate growled, as Clay's car swung into the tight country lanes both with ease and speed. "I simply said I'm glad I got through to him the other week." He smiled smugly. "And Dr. Jakes said the same thing yesterday. She was quite impressed at my teenage handling skills."

He swore as Clay avoided a dead badger in the road and narrowly missed the hedge on the opposite side. "Fuck, Clay, I can see why Taylor moans about Draven's driving. What the heck are you trying to do, kill us?"

"I went on another defensive driving course a couple of weeks ago." Out of the corner of his eyes, Clay sniggered as Tate's jaw tightened when the SUV bypassed a slow-moving tractor with only an inch to spare. "It's fun testing out my driving skills. And besides, this car is made for this sort of driving."

Testing out some newfound skills wasn't all Clay was doing. He'd also noticed a car that appeared to be following them, a dark grey BMW. His suspicions had been aroused as they'd gotten onto the motorway and the car had seemed to keep pace with them. Moving into the country lanes had been a great way to shake off a potential pursuer. He hadn't noticed the vehicle since he'd done that though so he was beginning to doubt his earlier suspicion. Perhaps he was simply being paranoid. It had been a long week.

He was also proud of himself for telling Tate about the BMW as well. There was no way Clay wanted a repeat of the last time he'd kept things from his lover.

"No car is made for your sort of driving," Tate muttered as his fingers tightened on the seat. "Christ, I thought going undercover was dangerous. It's nothing compared to this daredevil shit you're doing. Fuck, Clay, can you watch where you're going? Can we get back on the motorway?" He glanced behind them. "I don't see anyone following us now. Maybe the guy was just out for a drive in his fancy car."

Clay chuckled as he slid the Audi between a slow-moving white van and a dip in the road, which would have meant a broken axle or worse had they gone in. "Stop being such a damn baby. I know what I'm doing. I'm a trained professional."

"Smug bastard," Tate groaned, looking a little green.

Clay grinned. "Well, you wanted to come with…" he pointed out slyly.

There had been a break in the case that Clay was working on with the police regarding the toxic waste dumping. A call had come in to his office, been verified by his team and now he and Tate were on their way to Oxford to meet with some local government councillor. The man said he'd gotten the evidence that toxic chemicals *were* being illegally dumped in the old quarry and had the names of those involved.

Clay's missing person hadn't made an appearance yet and Clay hoped that this lead would check out and point him in the right direction to the missing Glen Walkerman, who Clay believed was the kingpin behind the multi-million-pound illegal activities. He also believed Walkerman was a killer.

Tate glared at him. "You offered me an overnight stay in a quaint little bed and breakfast in the heart of Chipping Norton in the Cotswolds afterwards. I fancied the idea of having an intimate rendezvous with you, away from home. Bite me."

"Maybe later…" Clay drawled and laughed as Tate muttered something intelligible. He did have a faint smile on his face and Clay went warm thinking about what might be in store for him later. He could definitely use Tate's talented mouth around his dick…and on his lips.

The warm July air rushed through his window. The scent of warm grass and Tate's aftershave gave Clay a good feeling—until he saw the familiar headlights and number plate in his rearview mirror. The car was closing fast and didn't look as if it was about to slow down. "Fuck," he swore, casting a quick glance at Tate to make sure he had his seatbelt on. "That BMW is behind us again. I knew I wasn't imagining it."

Tate's eyes widened and he turned to stare behind at the rapidly approaching car.

"It's the same one," he said quietly, nodding. "Can you outrun him? Looks like he intends ramming us."

Not for the first time Clay blessed having a fellow law enforcement officer as a partner who was quick to catch on and didn't ask unnecessary questions or freak out.

He grinned. "This guy doesn't know who he's messing with. If he wants to fuck with me, he'd better be prepared to get fucked in return." He sped up and widened the distance between the cars. The lanes were narrow and winding and Clay hoped to God there wasn't much traffic ahead. The last thing he wanted was to get innocent people hurt.

"I'll try find somewhere to pull over rather than take this on the roads." His eyes flicked back to the mirror. The BMW was gaining on them again. "We might have to shoot our way out of this one."

Tate nodded as he opened the glove compartment and took out Clay's Colt .38 revolver. It was a Detective Special, a piece Clay swore by.

"I'm ready," Tate said grimly. "You drive, I'll shoot. Maybe we can get this fucker before too much damage happens." His jaw clenched as he checked the weapon.

Danger and the resulting adrenaline were always a turn-on for Clay. His cock jumped in his chinos at Tate's tight jaw and the fierce look in his hazel eyes. "I love the way you think."

God, the man looks sexy with that gun in his hand. Definitely going to do me some role play soon. Excellent time to be thinking with your little head, Clay. Focus.

"You're thinking about sex, aren't you?" Tate murmured, his eyes drawn to Clay's groin. "I can't believe you just sprang a boner. You like seeing me with a gun." He smirked and then it changed to quiet determination as he glanced behind them. "He's pretty close, Clay. We need to get off this damn road in case someone innocent gets hurt."

"I know." Clay gritted his teeth and floored the accelerator. The Audi shot ahead but the BMW must have been souped up; it kept pace with Clay's vehicle no matter what he did. Ahead, the road twisted to a blind bend. Then the BMW rammed into them.

Both of them swore loudly. Tate gripped the dashboard and the gun as he glanced behind. Clay tightened his grip on the wheel and tried to keep control as the BMW rammed them again. His eyes assessed the situation ahead in an instant.

So far no traffic. Trees either side, embankments a few feet high, no room to pull off. Just got to keep going and hope we don't encounter any other cars.

Tate twisted around in his seat. "I need to shoot this arsehole. Give him something to think about. Slow him down." He looked down at the seatbelt restricting his movement.

Clay shook his head vehemently. "Don't you fucking dare take that off," he commanded as he strove to drive faster. "If we crash, I don't need you flying through the damn windshield."

"It's not giving me much of a damn shot, Clay." Tate snarled. He managed to get the seatbelt slack enough to turn on his seat and kneel, looking behind him. He positioned himself between the seats and aimed as the vehicle careened around another bend. Clay heard Tate swear, heard the fire of the gun and the shattering of the Audi's rear windscreen. Tate fired another shot, then another. Clay had no way of knowing whether any of the shots were hitting their target. He hoped one of them would blow the pursuer's head off.

"Got him," The triumphant satisfaction in Tate's voice was hard to miss. "At least it went through his damn windscreen. I think he's intact, more's the pity."

The BMW rammed them again, at a different angle and the Audi went sideways, wheels spinning in the dirt of the foliage-covered embankment.

"Christ, Tate, hold on." Clay shouted as he battled with the steering. Thankfully the car remained on all four wheels and righted itself. The road opened a little wider and Clay saw his chance. He geared down and braked suddenly, the loss of momentum causing Tate to cry out in surprise. The BMW hadn't seen that coming either and drew almost level with the Audi. Clay thrummed the engine and rammed the other car side on, driving it against the embankment. He pulled away and did it again. The screeching of tyres from the BMW as the driver struggled to control it was music to Clay's ears.

"Let's see how you like that, you bastard," he snarled. "Fuck with me and mine and I *will* hurt you."

The BMW looked as if it was having trouble staying on the road and Clay rammed it again for good measure. The road opened into fields lined with huge trees and as Clay went back in for the kill, Tate fired off another shot from his position. There was a loud pop and one of the BMW's tyres burst. It lost traction and as Tate and

Clay watched, the car slid off the road and plowed head-on into the trunk of a tree. Both men growled in victory at the grinding noise and resultant smash, but they had more important things to focus on than satisfaction. Clay's own vehicle was all over the road and as he geared down, trying to right the Audi and slow it down, he heard Tate's panicked roar.

"Jesus, Clay, watch out for that damned cyclist. You're heading straight for him!"

Clay glanced to the side and was confronted with the vision of a red helmet and someone on the side of the road on a bike. He swung the steering wheel urgently, trying to move away from the cyclist. The manoeuvre caused the car to slip wildly across the road, hit a ditch, bounce in the air then flip sideways.

We're going to fucking roll.

Clay shouted a warning to Tate. He instinctively reached out, letting go of the steering wheel with his left hand, using that arm across the front of Tate's chest as a brace. Clay knew that that was a worthless gesture given the circumstances, but like a mother with her child, his first thought was to protect his boyfriend. Then the vehicle went arse over bonnet into green fields covered in purple flowers, and Clay's head hit the doorframe as everything went dark.

****

Throbbing head. Eyes glued together with something sticky, a pain in his shoulder that made his eyes water and an overwhelming silence.

Clay groaned and moved his hand toward the passenger seat. Immediately a stab of pain shot through his left shoulder. He gritted his teeth and reached out again, ignoring the agony. "Tate? Are you okay?" Nausea rose in Clay's throat and he coughed, trying to get rid of the taste of blood. "Tate?" There was no response and Clay fumbled around as best he could with his right arm, trying to unhook his seat belt. His body throbbed with pain, his head more so, but he persevered.

I have to get to Tate. God, please let him be all right.

Finally there was the welcome sound of a click and the seatbelt drew back. Clay struggled upright from the position he was in. The car had landed upside down, and his boyfriend lay motionless beside him, blood trickling from his mouth, eyes closed. Panic set in as Clay pushed at his door with his feet, biting back a cry of pain as something in his leg protested.

"Hold on, the ambulance is on its way." A woman's voice floated in through the pain and as Clay finally kicked the door open, a hand reached down and gripped his. "Let me help you. Then we can get your friend out."

Clay nodded and between them, they managed to extricate him from the wreck of his car. The woman, still in her cyclist helmet, stared at him with concerned blue eyes. "Is everything okay? I was trying to get the door open myself but it was stuck and I couldn't manage it."

Clay heaved a shuddering sigh as he checked himself for damage. "Yes, I think I'm fine. Bruised and I have a helluva headache, but I'll live." He moved around to the Tate's side of the car. "I need to check on my boyfriend. He doesn't look too good."

Heart racing, he pulled at the door. It was jammed and Clay lost it. "Bloody fucking hell," he snarled as he pulled and kicked it. "Tate, love, please talk to me. I'm trying to get you out—just hold on."

There was a low groan from inside the car. "Shit, this is a cluster fuck of note." Tate sounded really pissed off.

Clay laughed with relief. "Just hold on. I'm going to get you out of there."

He pulled at the door as the cyclist took hold of it with him and together they managed to wrench it open. In the distance Clay heard sirens.

"Sounds like the cavalry is here, so hold on. Let me get that damn seatbelt off then we can get you out."

"Better hurry. I can smell fuel and I don't fancy being a crispy critter." Tate's voice was husky and he coughed. Clay saw the wince of pain cross Tate's face as Clay tried to free his lover.

Clay's fingers worked the seatbelt loose and then, between he and the woman, they managed to get Tate out of the car and well away from it lest it explode. Clay didn't think it was a possibility despite the smell of fuel, but better safe than sorry.

Tate looked battered and bruised, had a split lip and a rather nasty rip to the flesh at his collarbone. From the looks of him and the way he moved, Clay thought he might have damaged ribs as well.

"I'm fine," Tate said tiredly as Clay checked him out again. "How are you? That head wound of yours looks nasty."

The woman shook her head. "It's just a flesh wound. I checked your boyfriend out already. I'm a nurse. My name's Anne." She smiled at them both. "Thanks for not riding me down, by the way. I'm sorry you had to crash to avoid me. What happened? Did you serve to miss something?"

Clay snorted. "No. Some arsehole tried to ram us off the road. He crashed a little ways back." He looked at Tate. "Speaking of which, I want to go see what happened to him. I'll be back in a minute."

Anne's startled gasp of horror made Tate smile tiredly and he waved at Clay. "Go. I'll tell Anne here all about it." The sirens grew closer. "Sounds like they're nearly here." He cast a dire look in Clay's direction. "Not that I'm going anywhere with them."

Clay rolled his eyes. "You could do with checking out."

"I'll go if you go," Tate said mutinously. "Otherwise forget it. I hate fucking hospitals."

"Fine," Clay muttered in exasperation as he turned and walked down toward the smashed car in the distance. "Bloody stubborn git."

His leg ached, his back ached, and the little people in his head were trying to tunnel out of his skull to the surface using pickaxes, but Clay was grateful neither he nor Tate was badly injured. He couldn't say the same about the man in the BMW once he reached the vehicle. Clay knew he wasn't supposed to be scrabbling around in a dead man's pockets trying to find out who he was, but the guy wasn't going to be going anywhere. His neck was broken, his skull crushed and Clay's sense of justice was mollified.

"Try to kill me and my man, and you'll end up second best," he murmured to the body as he rifled his pockets, anxious to do it before the police and ambulances arrived. He gave a hiss of satisfaction when he found the man's wallet and driving licence.

"Well, Mr Glen Walkerman, I guess I found you. Pity the cops won't be able to put you away in prison but I guess dead fits just as well. Bastard." Clay knew he sounded callous, but the man lying with open eyes in the car before him had killed two people and just tried to kill two more. Clay was in no mood to be sympathetic.

He trudged back to the scene of his accident, having wiped down the wallet—just in case—and removed all traces of himself from the BMW. Tate raised an eyebrow at him as he sat on the ground.

"Our guy is no longer missing, or alive," Clay said grimly. "I'm guessing he thought ramming us off the road, maiming us would slow us down or kill us so he could get to the guy we were going to see." He waved his mobile. "I already called the team and asked them to make sure the council guy is kept safe. Bring him in for questioning. He obviously has something worth telling."

Tate shrugged. "One less villain in the world to worry about if Walkerman's dead."

Both of them watched as the ambulance and two police cars pulled up. Anne was closer and she approached them, gesticulating wildly, obviously explaining what had happened.

"She's a nice woman," Tate said softly. He grinned. "Very happy we didn't pulverise her into a hedge like bramble jelly. Her words, not mine."

Clay laughed as he stretched, trying to ease the kinks out of his body. "I guess we have a lot of explaining to do," he sighed. "This is going to be fun." He cast a jaundiced eye at his SUV. "And that's a fucking write-off. I s'pose I have an excuse to buy a new one now. A faster one."

Tate groaned, no doubt hearing the relish in Clay's tone. "Really? Like this"—he waved at the mess in the road—"wasn't enough for Mr Adrenaline Junkie?" He winced and held his ribs. Clay sat down beside him and draped an aching arm over his shoulders.

"I'm just glad we made it out of that wreck," he said quietly. "I'm glad we can sit here together and laugh about it. I don't know what I would do if anything happened to you."

Tate smiled at him, his agreement obvious beneath the pain. "Ditto." His eyes narrowed as a paramedic walked toward them. "Heads up. Looks like we're going on a ride."

Clay turned to look at the paramedic and sighed. "Yep. I guess we're both going to get checked out at the hospital if that's the only way I can get you to go. No doubt the cops will be there too, wanting an explanation. Especially with the dead guy down the road and the bullet holes." He leaned over and kissed Tate gently on the lips. "Sorry we won't get that romantic night away. Looks like we're going to be busy for a while."

Chapter 13

Tate lay in bed at Clay's house, the warmth of the duvet on his naked body a welcome solace to his aching bones and limbs. They'd both been patched up at the hospital; Tate had bruised ribs, a couple of stitches in the torn flesh of his shoulder and a swollen lip. Clay had a nasty gash in his head, which had required cleaning and taping and not much else. Both men knew they'd been past lucky.

Tate settled down with a sigh into Clay's king-sized bed. It had been the afternoon from hell what with the accident and then the myriad questions at the hospital and police station. The dead man had definitely been a complication. Thanks to some eyewitness testimony from a young couple who'd been parked in the woods making out, heard the noise and seen the BMW's blowout, it looked like he and Clay were off the hook as far as actually causing his death. The bullet holes and shattered front windscreen had of course taken some explaining, but Tate had managed to impart that it had been purely in self-defence. There was probably still a little fallout to come, but both Tate and Clay were confident that they'd weather that storm, given the connection to the Met case and Rick's intervention.

The car had been towed off but was probably a write off. It looked like Clay would definitely be getting a shiny new toy.

Tate was still edgy. They could have lost each other today and for Tate that was a scenario that he couldn't accept. Life without Clay in it meant nothing.

His skin prickled as if being teased with tiny surges of electricity that ebbed and flowed as he moved. His legs couldn't keep still, moving restlessly beneath the covers. His dick ached, hard and needy. He tried taking a few deep breaths to calm the raging soul inside him, but it didn't appear to be helping. And when Clay came into the room, dressed in boxers, the dark hair on both his head and chest matted with moisture from the shower, Tate's cock immediately took notice. He growled softly and Clay's eyes narrowed, his lips curving in a soft grin as he observed the rapidly tenting cover under which Tate lay.

"Feeling agitated? Danger does that to a man," Clay murmured as he slipped his thumbs into his boxers and slid them off. He threw them onto the rattan chair in the corner as he regarded Tate with heated eyes.

Tate's cock hardened further at the sight of Clay's own hard-on, and the fine line of hair leading down to his dark-haired groin. Clay's toned stomach contracted and tensed as he moved, flat planes of skin and golden muscles that Tate wanted to bite and ravage with his mouth and teeth.

Clay chuckled softly. "No need to ask what you're thinking about." He lifted the cover and got in beside Tate, pulling the duvet down over their waists. His warm legs pressed against Tate's, the touch of heated skin and flesh against flesh making a seductive sound. "Are you up to this now? I know you bruised your ribs, and that cut on your shoulder doesn't need to start bleeding again." Clay grimaced. "My head is feeling better, but it still aches like shit."

At this stage, Tate really didn't care about his injuries. He'd taken his painkillers. Right now, all he wanted was Clay. If truth be told, he was having a little trouble breathing, his need and desire to fuck so strong he wasn't sure he'd be able to control himself from literally riding Clay's dick there and then, lube and aches and pains be damned. He was as horny as Hellboy, no doubt from the adrenaline residue in his blood and the knowledge that they both could have been killed today.

He shook his head as he pulled the duvet off their bodies and swung his legs over to straddle Clay's hips. His balls made contact with the tight skin of Clay's lower stomach and he hissed in pleasure at the sensation.

"No time for thinking, only fucking," he moaned as he leant down and violently took Clay's mouth in a kiss that made them both gasp in pleasure. Tate tasted blood from his split lip and probably from where one of his teeth had nipped Clay's lips. Emboldened by the taste of blood and the pain, he thrust his tongue into Clay's mouth roughly, tasting his man, feeling the wetness of his mouth against his.

The noise Clay made, part growl, part groan made Tate harder than he thought he'd ever felt in his life.

"Christ, I am going to come just like this," he groaned, as his wet, swollen cock pushed against the bare skin of Clay's stomach. "I'm just so damn turned on, I can't think—"

He gave a moan of frustration as Clay's mouth left his but his disappointment was soon overshadowed when strong hands gripped his hips, fingers digging deep, hurting, and no doubt bruising his flesh.

"Up on your hands and knees, over me," Clay growled hoarsely. "I need to feel my fingers inside you, opening you so you can ride my cock. Want to split you open." He reached under the pillow for the tube of lube. Tate's heart stuttered as Clay opened it and squeezed fluid onto his fingers. His balls contracted and he nodded desperately, the sight of Clay's pupils, black and dilated, the snarl of ferocity on his face nearly undoing him.

"Yes," Tate panted as he did what he'd been commanded. He leaned forward, placing his hands on either side of Clay's waist and leaned over so Clay had easier access to the eager hole. "Need to feel you in me. First your fingers then that big, beautiful cock of yours. Want to ride you 'til I can't think."

Clay snarled and thrust his fingers deeply into Tate, pushing and twisting Tate's hole until he cried out. As he loomed above Clay, half lying, half sitting over his body, the feeling of those rough fingers inside him was exactly what he needed. As Clay opened Tate up, his other hand gripped Tate's jaw and pulled his mouth down to his. Lips and teeth ground together and both men moaned in pain and pleasure. Tate's cock was squashed against Clay's flesh, every move causing friction and he cried out as the slick wetness of his pre-come coated Clay's stomach and left trails of white across Clay's belly.

"Don't come yet," Clay commanded him, his lips glistening and swollen, eyes darkened with passion. He made another fierce twist inside Tate's arse. "You wait for me to be inside you before you do that."

Tate hitched a deep breath. "God, you bastard, then I suggest you fuck me sooner rather than later. Because I am going to come so damn hard in a minute."

Clay's face flushed and his teeth bit down none too gently on Tate's jaw, causing him to yip in pain. "Then do it. Now."

Tate needed no further urging. He lifted himself up, trying to ignore the pain in his battered body, and stared down at the man who half sat, half lay beneath him. Clay's face was twisted in lust and want, and his cock jutted proudly from the thatch of dark curls at his groin. Tate bit his lip and then lowered himself down onto the hot, slick and eager dick waiting for him. Clay's deep gasp of satisfaction made his hole throb, as did the burn of Clay in his arse. Tate spread his legs to take Clay deeper then began to slowly move above him, his hips undulating and his inner muscles tightening around Clay's cock.

The feeling of power he got from watching his lover slowly lose it was like nothing else. That Tate could take such control of this man he loved, that he could watch his self-control unravel like a skein of wool—that was something for a man to be proud of.

As Tate rose and fell, his hands resting behind him on Clay's strong thighs, Clay's cock sliding in and out of him, he revelled in the primal urge to be impaled and fucked to destruction. He was flying so high, the bruised ribs and plastered-up shoulder were of no consequence.

Huh. Sexual endorphins make for great painkillers.

Tate's inflamed cock had no chance when Clay's hand wrapped around it. It took barely three pulls before he was crying out, shooting ribbons of come over Clay's belly and chest, his muscles tensing around Clay's cock as he climaxed. The feeling of Clay's own orgasm, the hot, sudden heat filling Tate's tender passage and Clay's hoarse grunts as his hips thrust upward—it appeared nirvana was here and now.

Tate had found his paradise in the scent of sweat and semen, and the soft exhalations of his lover as he spent himself inside him. He leaned down, still feeling Clay inside him. Tate pressed fevered, dry lips to Clay's, wanting to breathe him in, taste him—own him.

Fuck, I want to consume him.

For a while, the only sound in the room was the soft fleshy smack of lips, mewls of pleasure as both men strove to absorb the other. Finally, needing to breathe himself, Tate released Clay's mouth and smiled as he stared down at the thoroughly debauched sight before him.

"You look like you've been well and truly fucked," he muttered softly. Clay's lips were red and bitten and there was a small smear of come on his jaw. Tate leaned down and licked it off. "I'm sure I look the same. My arse is damn sore."

He knelt up and uncoupled himself from Clay's sticky groin. Between his cheeks and down his legs, Tate felt and smelt Clay's come and he smiled to himself. He reached down and wiped a bit of Clay's spunk off his thighs then slowly, teasingly, he painted Clay's lips with it. Clay's eyes grew blacker and he made a noise that sounded like a snarl. Tate was ready for a second round there and then with that sexy noise.

"Love it when you claim me like that," he whispered as Clay's hand reached out and he pulled Tate's fingers into his mouth, sucking them, his eyes never leaving Tate's.

"You are mine, Tate. Never forget that." Clay flipped Tate onto his back and held Tate's hands above his head with one hand as the other found its way down to Tate's arsehole. Tate lost his breath at the expression of possession in Clay's eyes. His prick ached as he grew hard again.

Clay's fingers pushed gently into Tate's sensitive hole and he held his breath as Clay scooped up his own come from Tate's arse. He opened his mouth instinctively then Clay's fingers pushed into his mouth, smelling of musk and his own sex. Tate swallowed down what he was being given, the taste and scent of Clay arousing his senses and his cock again.

"This is my spunk inside you, and in your mouth," Clay whispered, "*proving* you're mine." Clay bit down on Tate's ear as he watched Tate sucking his fingers. His hardness pressed against Tate's stomach again. "We took long enough to get here, to this point, you here with me. I don't ever intend losing you. I could have lost you today and that scares the shit out of me. I don't ever want a life where you aren't in it."

"I know," Tate whispered as he licked the final bit of Clay off the fingers in his mouth. He pulled his hands free from Clay's grip, desperate to touch the man in his arms. "I feel the same way. I need you. You're mine as much as I'm yours. Remember that too."

Clay nodded, green eyes staring at Tate with tenderness. "I'll never forget that. Count on it."

Tate felt those eyes on him as he padded naked to the bathroom to get a bunch of industrial-strength wet wipes. When he got back to the bed, he handed some to Clay and they cleaned themselves up. Tate took the used ones and wadded them into the rubbish bin. Then he got back into bed and snuggled himself into Clay's arms, head on his lover's shoulder.

"How are your ribs?" Clay stroked a hand over his hair, fingers caressing his forehead.

Tate waggled a languid hand. "Sore. I'll live." He chuckled softly. "How's the headache, dear? Do you need an aspirin?"

Clay snorted tiredly. "Shut up. Like you, I'll live. Sleep will do me the world of good." His voice already sounded sleepy. He yawned widely.

Tate couldn't help but yawn too. He closed his eyes and trailed his fingers gently over Clay's lavender wipe-fragranced stomach. "I'm glad we got out of that mess okay today. It could have been nasty."

Clay nodded drowsily. "You were awesome with that gun though. So damn badass. It fucking turned me on, danger or not."

"Yeah? You liked that? Maybe we need to role play. Cop and villain. You can bend me over the interrogation table and fuck me when I don't tell you the truth."

"Jesus, Tate, don't say things like that just when we're both so exhausted. I don't need another boner when I'm trying to get to sleep."

The smile in his lover's voice warmed Tate. He grinned against Clay's skin. "I see me with my trousers down round my ankles, arse in the air just begging for it, you wearing my old uniform trousers, unzipped, your big, thick cock pushing out, and then you push me facedown onto the table and ram into me—"

His words were broken off as Clay's hand clamped down over his mouth.

"Enough, you bastard. Go to sleep. Hell, I'm sporting wood now." Clay's voice was aggrieved. "How am I supposed to sleep like this? Arsehole…oh hell, that feels good."

Tate grinned as he wrapped his hand around Clay's semi-hardened dick and took his mouth in a dirty, open mouthed kiss. His man's recovery time was admirable and a hand job before bed was a definite sleeping tablet in his book.

****

Clay emptied the coffee refill into the jar as he waited for the kettle to boil. He moved the two coffee cups around the kitchen top as if playing a game of cups and balls. The feeling of nervousness that had plagued him since he'd made up his mind two days ago to do what he was about to do was still there. He could make life-or-death decisions in an instant but something like asking Tate to move in with him permanently was freaking him out.

He shook his head ruefully then grimaced at the pain. Hangovers were not conducive to rapid head movements. Luckily he and Tate were recovered from their car accident, and the last two weeks had been fairly normal as their lives went. Clay's part in the toxic dumping affair was over. He'd found the man *he* was looking for and now it was up to the police to see what they could do with the remnants of the case. Their informant had been taken into protective custody and the whole toxic waste dump affair was unfolding like a concertina.

He stared out at the wild garden of his backyard. He hadn't had much time lately to maintain it and it was looking overgrown—beautifully tangled and wild, but still overrun with thistles and weeds.

He turned as Tate came into the kitchen, dressed in tight green briefs and an open white shirt. His hair was growing and what had once been a close buzz cut was now more a spiky auburn mess, a mess Clay really liked. It made Tate look younger, more vulnerable and less like the hard-arsed undercover agent he'd once been. Hazel eyes crinkled in welcome as Tate saw Clay standing there.

"I could die for coffee," Tate said, throat still husky no doubt from the deep throating he'd done last night. He and Clay had come home last night from a visit to Rick and his girlfriend, where they enjoyed a dinner worthy of Gordon Ramsay, but without the foul language. They'd also drunk far too much, and had stumbled into Clay's place in a veritable fit of giggles at something they'd seen or heard on the way home that had seemed hilarious at the time but in the stark light of day, probably hadn't been. In fact, Clay couldn't even remember now what had been so damned funny.

Whatever it was, Tate had been determined that he could 'buck the trend' and decided to swallow Clay's cock the minute he'd gotten home—with gusto. Tate was particularly skilled at blow jobs, having an impressive ability to take Clay deep—a favour Clay wasn't able to quite return although he didn't do too badly, thank you very much.

"You sound a bit rough," Clay smirked as he made Tate his coffee, strong and black.

Tate snorted. "Yeah, well, what the hell was I bloody thinking last night? I definitely had one too many tequila shots."

Clay nodded. "I think we both did. And what the hell did we think was so funny you had to prove you could stick my dick down your throat until it reached your stomach?"

The two men stared at each other in bemusement for a while, trying to recall the memory then burst out laughing. Clay lost his breath both with his own laughter and his sheer relief at the sound of Tate's. It had been a long time since he'd heard his lover make that incredibly infectious noise, a mix of belly laughter and snorting at the same time. Finally, the hilarity ceased and they both wiped their eyes and picked up their coffee cups.

"I guess we'll never know," Tate chuckled with a teasing glance at Clay's crotch. "I guess as long as you, me and Clayzilla down there enjoyed it, there's no harm done." He took a sip of his drink.

"Oh, it was definitely enjoyable," Clay murmured. "And honestly—*Clayzilla*?" Tate's snigger of amusement was cut off by Clay leaning in and taking his lover's mouth in a deep, coffee-tasting, good-morning kiss. Tate's breath and his low moan into Clay's mouth clearly made Clayzilla happy too.

They were interrupted in their tongue calisthenics by the ringing of Tate's mobile phone.

They unglued their mouths and Tate swore. "Christ, it's only nine on a Saturday morning." Tate reached over and picked up his phone. "It's Rick," he answered. "Rick, you just interrupted morning sex with my man. You'd better have a damn good reason for calling me this early." He winked at Clay who chuckled. There was a loud squawking on the other side of the phone.

Tate rolled his eyes. "What do you mean, TMI? You've never had morning sex? You don't know what you're missing. It's the best time to make use of morning wood."

Clay shook his head in amusement as the squawking grew louder. "Stop baiting him," he whispered with a snigger. "The man's going to have serious issues."

He frowned as Tate's face darkened and his mouth slid into a tight line at whatever Rick was now saying.

Something was wrong.

Clay took another gulp of his sweet, strong coffee and watched the rest of the conversation play out. Emotions rippled across his boyfriend's face—sadness, anger and resignation all appearing. Some minutes later, Tate sighed and passed a hand over his eyes.

"Yeah, thanks for telling me. I 'preciate it. Tell that sister of mine I say hi and it's time we got together for that roast dinner she promised me."

Rick rang off; Tate put his phone down and turned to face Clay. His face was set, a trace of sadness on it.

"What is it?" Clay asked softly.

"They found out who Lily really was," Tate said quietly. "And it's not a pretty story." He picked up his coffee cup, made a face and then put it down. "Her real name was Amy Knight. She was fourteen years old and had been on the streets for about a year."

Clay reached over and placed his hand on Tate's. "That's shitty, being on your own like that. What else did Rick say?"

Tate huffed, his eyes distant. "It's a bit stereotypical really. She had an argument with her parents about her not being able to see some boy, got the hump in and ran away from home. They never saw her again. They'd been trying to find her but it wasn't until her picture appeared in a local newspaper up north that they recognised her. They contacted Rick yesterday and drove down from Manchester to identify her body. How she managed to get to London is anyone's guess. Her mother told Rick she had an online friend down this way—perhaps she was trying to find her. We'll never know."

Tate stared at Clay with troubled eyes. "Apparently she was quite a regular at the clinic down the road, not far from where I met her." His face tightened and the welling emotion was evident in his face. "She was treated for various STDs and pneumonia. She was coughing blood when I saw her." He went silent and Clay saw the pain in his eyes when he looked up. "When she died, she was also six weeks pregnant."

Clay's stomach lurched. "Christ, that poor kid, and the baby. Stupid question I know, but do they have any idea who the father might have been?"

Tate shrugged. His body language made Clay want to pull him close and never let go. He wasn't sure that was what Tate wanted right now so he held off.

"They have no idea. I doubt they'll try and find out either." Tate's hands clenched. "She stood no fucking chance. She was young and vulnerable and chose to kill herself because she was in trouble, with nowhere to go." His voice thickened with rage. "If I ever find out who made her pregnant, I'll bloody well kill them."

"You think she knew that she was pregnant?" Clay asked softly as he ran a finger down the side of Tate's fisted hand.

Tate nodded. "She said something about it being too late for either of them. At the time I didn't understand." He stopped then blurted out, his expression anguished, "I should have nagged her more. I should have made her go to that damned hospital."

And now it was time for Clay to pull his tormented lover into his arms and murmur words of comfort in his ear. "Baby, you did what you could. There's only so much you can do for someone. You're spending time at Castaways trying to help kids who need it, that's something. Those kids love you like a big brother from what Dr Jakes told us in our sessions. So please don't let this one thing fester inside of you. You need to let it go."

Inside Clay raged that each step forward that Tate took, there always seemed to be a step backward attached to it. Some sort of piss-poor karma delivered by a fate that loved playing sick jokes on people who were already hurting.

Clay held Tate close for a while as they both stared out into the unruly garden and watched the next-door cat try and catch an unsuspecting sparrow. The sparrow realised its vulnerability at the last minute and eluded the cat with an indignant chirp.

"It's looking like damn Borneo out there," Tate muttered as he pulled away from Clay. "We need to get a gardener in here and get it seen to before the tigers breed and eat us in our beds."

Clay chuckled softly. "I don't believe there are any tigers in Borneo. Some civets maybe and definitely orang-utans." He was glad Tate appeared to have taken his advice on board. Time, however, would tell how far *that* went. His man was a stubborn as hell. It was what had kept him alive in the past.

Tate gave him a look of disdain. "Listen to you, David Attenborough. Mr bloody know it all." But his soft grin took the sting out of his words.

Clay cleared his throat. "Speaking of the garden. I'm glad you said 'we.' There's something I've been meaning to speak to you about."

Tate's face flushed. "Sorry, when I said 'we' I obviously meant you. I mean it's your house."

Clay ran a hand down Tate's cheek. "Unless you want it to be *our* house. I'm up for that if you are."

Tate's eyes widened. "What are you saying?"

Clay scratched his head. How come this was so damned awkward?

"I mean maybe you want to move in here. You're here most of the time anyway, and half your clobber is in my spare room. So now we're out and proud, and everyone knows about our relationship, and I've stopped being such a protective Daddy Bear, then I thought perhaps..." his voice tailed off. Tate's face was a picture in...something...and Clay wasn't sure whether it was good or bad. His boyfriend hid his eyes behind his arm and his body shook. Clay was a little peeved. It looked like Tate was laughing and Clay didn't think the request was that funny.

"What the hell is so damn amusing?" he growled, his pride a little hurt.

Tate snorted as he moved his arm away and his eyes shone with mirth. "Protective *Daddy Bear*? Oh my God." He collapsed in a fit of giggling. "And yes, you crazy bastard. I'll move in with you." His eyes softened. "I thought you'd never ask."

Clay grinned his heart filling with both relief and joy. Tate never giggled. This was pretty new and he liked it.

"Yes," Clay purred, moving toward Tate and gripping his hips, pulling him against his body. "All the better to eat you with, or however that damn fairy tale goes. Or was that something else? I'm not very good with fairy tales."

Tate was still chuckling when Clay hefted him onto his shoulder and took him into the bedroom where he proceeded to show the man writhing eagerly beneath him exactly how a Daddy Bear ate someone.

Chapter 14

Galileo's buzzed with activity as Clay walked back from the bar
with a round of drinks. His friends were all seated in a corner booth,
chatting animatedly. He grinned at Tate who already looked a little
under the weather as he tried to convince Eddie of the benefits of
briefs versus boxers. Eddie gave Clay a 'please help me' puppy dog
look which Clay ignored. He knew exactly what happened when
Tate got onto that subject, Clay being a boxer man himself, and he
didn't want to get involved. He smothered a laugh as he sat down
and heard the words 'dangling junk' seeing Eddie's panicked look
around the restaurant to check if anyone else had heard Tate's rather
loud ode to the delights of wearing briefs to keep his junk
"contained."

Taylor waved his beer bottle in Clay's direction. "More booze.
Just what we needed." He slugged down the remains of his current
drink and picked up another one.

His fiancé, Draven, sighed. "Tay, remember what happened the
last time you got drunk? You gave Tate hell, and then it ended up
with Gideon politely kicking you and me out of the restaurant with
poor Clay as the babysitter."

Clay laughed loudly. "I remember that night well. I thought
poor Gideon was going to pitch a fit."

"Poor Gideon *did* pitch a fit," was the dry rejoinder from behind
and Clay turned to see the man in question standing there. He was
immaculately clad as always in a grey suit, as befitted the owner of
Galileo's. He sat down in the empty chair beside Eddie and leaned
over to kiss his cheek.

Gideon grinned. "If I recall, it was a bit like the Nicky Starr
porn site in here that night." He frowned. "Talking about Oliver and
Leslie, weren't they supposed to be here?"

Taylor nodded. "Yep. Something happened to one of Leslie's
fish—again—so poor Oliver had to go around and console him.
They'll be a bit late."

Eddie laughed loudly. "If by *console*, you mean that Oliver had
to go round and flush the little fishy tyke down the toilet because
Leslie was in hysterics and couldn't do it, you hit it on the head." He

grimaced. "I don't know what it is with that man and his pets. He has this nasty habit of losing them."

Draven shook his head in amusement. "I bet that's not all that's getting *consoled*," he said slyly.

The table burst into raucous laughter. Clay chuckled at the merriment and thought not for the first time what a great bunch of people he had the pleasure of knowing. His relationship with Tate and Draven had brought him into contact with men he was really proud to call friends. The fact Tate had also agreed to move in with him made it even better. There was quite a bit to organise in terms of the move, but the fact that *his man* was going to be living with him definitely made the evening better.

Tate raised his drink at him and the warmth in those hazel eyes made Clay smile. His lover looked more relaxed than he'd seen him in a long while. That was partially down to the therapy he still underwent and Tate's unburdening of himself to Clay. He was so proud of Tate in coming to terms with his demons, he could burst.

Draven leaned over and touched his arm. "Tate is looking great," he murmured softly. "I'm so pleased for you both. I know you both went through a lot and to see him like this—it's pretty admirable. He's one tough bastard, isn't he?"

"That he is," Clay remarked fondly, watching and listening as Tate told some dirty joke about a penguin and a dwarf nun. He winced at the punchline. "God, that was a bit sexist even for him."

"That's what comes of working with misogynistic bastards like Sonny Armerian," Draven mused. "So big on proving they don't suck dick, they treat women like objects." He chuckled. "I guess in Tate's case, you can take the man out of the undercover cop—"

"But you can't take the undercover cop out of the man," they finished together and laughed.

Clay leaned in toward Draven. "I wanted to ask you how Taylor was," he murmured quietly as he watched the antics around the table. "You said he had a bit of a turn when we were in that accident—is everything okay now?"

Draven nodded, eyes on his fiancé. "Yeah, he was a bit under the weather for a while. Did the whole passing-out thing and shit." His lips twisted in a wry grin. "I guess it's all part of the fun of being involved with a psychic."

"But you wouldn't have it any other way," Clay said, nudging his friend's shoulder. "I know the feeling. Can't live with 'em; can't live without 'em." He glanced at Draven with a smirk. "I never thought I'd see the day Draven Samuels was in love. And yet here we are."

"Back atcha." Draven shot back. "And you, with Tate Williams? I never saw that one coming."

"Yeah, well." Clay shrugged. "We've known each other forever. We still take it day by day, but yeah. He'll be fine. Especially now he's moving in with me. I can keep an eye on him."

Both men shared a look that said they knew what it meant to take care of someone, even if the other person didn't really think they needed it. In their profession, protective instincts were a must.

A tornado in the form of Leslie Tiberius Scott chose that moment to make his entrance. Leslie was adept at making an entrance and Clay couldn't help but feel a surge of affection for the young man who'd manage to tame a former porn star and bring him out of hiding.

Oliver Brown, aka Nicky Starr in porn circles (and someone all of them had watched at some time or another) smirked at Taylor and Eddie as he sat down. "Sorry we're late," he announced, his hand reaching up and smoothing his hair over the scar Clay knew was there on his face. "Glenda died and we had to have the funeral there and then." He rolled his eyes and glanced fondly at his boyfriend.

Leslie pouted, brushing a stray lock of black hair away behind his ear. Despite the fact Clay had Tate, Clay thought Leslie was adorable.

"I wasn't going to let her sit around and be eaten by a cat or something," Leslie sputtered indignantly. "That damn tabby next door slipped into my flat the other day and ate all the salami I'd left out for my sandwich and I had to make do with boring ham. God knows what it would have done if it found Glenda lying in state. She'd have been gobbled up like that." He clicked his fingers and sat down.

Taylor and Eddie burst into loud fits of laughter.

"Leslie, did you just say a cat ate your salami? Oh my God, there has to be a joke in there somewhere." Taylor howled. He could always be counted on for a laugh, and Eddie wasn't much better. They nudged each other in mirth. Draven rolled his eyes and Gideon just shook his head. The two men shared a sympathetic glance at their respective partners' schoolboy humour.

Leslie glared at them, blue eyes flashing dangerously. "Ha-ha. You two are like dirty little kids, you know that?" He gave a smug grin. "Besides, my *salami's* too big to be eaten by a cat."

Eddie laughed louder. "Oh, please don't start on the whole eight-inches thing again."

Oliver leaned over the table with a grin. "Lads, my boyfriend's dick size is classed as need-to-know information. And you don't need to know." He smiled fondly at Leslie who batted his eyelashes back as he imperiously ordered his drink from the waitress.

The juvenile banter caused Clay a slight sense of insecurity. At the ripe age of thirty-six he was almost the daddy of the group. The thought irritated him and he scowled.

Tate leaned over and ran a hand down his jawline, warm eyes assessing him shrewdly. "Everything okay?" he murmured as his other hand caressed Clay's thigh under the table.

Clay sighed. "Just feeling like old Father Time," he admitted softly. "Look at this lot. I have about ten years on them all."

Tate snorted. "So do I when it comes to some of them. We're a right pair." His hand travelled further up Clay's leg and palmed his groin suggestively. "You are definitely sexy for an old bloke though." He squeezed hard and Clay tried not to make a noise as his dick hardened. He reached down and pushed Tate's hand off his crotch.

"Stop it," he hissed. "You start something and Gideon will throw us out." He cast a quick glance at the man in question but he was too busy kissing Eddie to hear them.

Tate chuckled and removed his hand. "Easy now, old-timer," he said, putting on a twang. "Don't go getting your panties in a bunch."

Clay snarled softly and reached across to grip Tate's jaw, loving the spark of lust and desire that flared there. "I'll show you who's not so damn old." He took Tate's mouth in a bruising kiss, owning him and forgetting for a moment just where they were. When they finally came up for air, both men realised the lack of conversation at the table.

"Oh. My. God," Leslie said, fanning himself with a menu. "That was so fucking hot!"

"Er, yeah, just a bit." Eddie's face was pink and he threw a heated glance at Gideon. "Pretty much a scorcher."

Both Gideon and Draven nodded in agreement. Taylor was too busy sitting with his mouth open to say anything, but from the dangerous look he flashed Draven, he had *something* on his mind.

Clay's face flamed. He'd never expected to be the centre of attention like this although it seemed they might just have contributed to everybody else's getting lucky later. For an *old-timer*, he was quite proud of that.

"Yeah, sorry," he said sheepishly as Tate snickered again and his hand crept up Clay's leg to the dick that was trying to punch its way out of his trousers. Clay gripped that wandering hand tightly.

God, my man is being such a prick tease tonight. I need to keep him away from alcohol when we're out. It does something to him, especially here at Galileo's.

Oliver grinned wolfishly. "If you guys fancy the idea, my old studio Vanguard is always looking for guys to perform for the more mature audience. I can give them a call if you like?"

The gleam in his eyes and the wicked twitch on his lips forestalled Clay's 'fuck you,' at that comment. Since meeting Leslie, Oliver had definitely come out of his hermit's shell. He'd proven to have a wicked sense of humour, a really dirty mind and knew every porn star in the business and their secrets, which kept them all entertained.

He was also clearly besotted with Leslie, but Clay didn't see how anyone could resist the blue-eyed minx. Everyone around the table had a great affection for him. He was the warm and fuzzy team mascot that got under your skin and you couldn't get him out.

Leslie gave a shriek of horror. "Babe, you can't say things like that to Clay and Tate." He smacked Oliver across the head with a menu. "Sorry, guys, Oliver sometimes has a big mouth."

The howl of laughter and Leslie's rapidly reddening cheeks at the dirty comments that followed, once again about the size of Leslie's cock, took the heat off Clay and Tate for a while.

When they finally left the restaurant, with the promise to all to arrange another 'Dirty Dinner' night, as Eddie had dubbed it, it was close to midnight. Clay definitely wanted to put the heat back into the bedroom. Tate had been a tease all night and now it was time for payback. And from the dangerous look in Tate's eyes, his lover was ready to pay the price.

****

Moving was a bitch but the results were worth it. Tate stared around the bedroom he now shared with Clay with a sense of accomplishment. He gave a nod of satisfaction and made his way to the patio. The French doors were open and a light, warm breeze blew in, caressing his face with tendrils of its warm breath. He stared out at the tangled garden with its overgrown foliage and unclipped greenery. It had been a hot and heavy weekend moving all his stuff out of his flat in Kentish Town into Clay's place, and putting some things into storage.

The past three weeks had been hectic to say the least. Organising removals, ensuring the utilities were stopped, changing his address, fobbing off his sister Lucy's offer of casseroles and stews (something Tate hated but Clay loved) and cleaning out the flat; it had taken a considerable amount of time.

Now he was firmly ensconced in a house he'd always considered home anyway. He loved Clay's huge Victorian house with its vineyard and peaceful garden. It bore so much of his partner—the classic wooden and leather study, with wall-to-wall books. The comfortable, old-style Quaker kitchen with its pale wood and centre island just perfect for eating around in the evenings. The ornate wrought-iron table and chairs on the private cobbled patio were perfect for warm summer evenings. It all spoke of warmth, safety and Clay.

Warm arms encircled him, pulling him against a strong, familiar body. Tate closed his eyes and breathed in Clay's beloved scent. Now, he *really* felt he was home.

"I'm wondering why the hell it took so long for us to get to this point," Clay whispered in his ear. "What the hell was I thinking—we could have done this a long time ago." He kissed the back of Tate's neck. "It was my fault, I know that. Me being all Daddy Bear and not wanting to risk you being hurt."

Tate reached back and pulled Clay's mouth down for a kiss. "You still make me laugh when you say that. Not to mention when I read 'Goldilocks' now I shall have really dirty thoughts." He turned and wrapped his arms around Clay's neck, laying his forehead against his. "Thank you for believing in me and staying with me after all the shit I've put you through." He pressed a finger to Clay's lips as he tried to speak. "Nope, be quiet. This is my turn to say important stuff." He smoothed a stray strand of Clay's hair from his cheek. "You inviting me into your home like this—it means everything to me. You once told me I was your world, your everything. Well, I need you to know I feel the same way. I love you, Clay Mortimer. To quote Mr Darren Hayes, 'Truly, Madly, Deeply.'" He grinned and saw Clay's eyes soften. "And the mind-blowing sex is good too."

Clay's chest rumbled as he laughed. "Good to know," he murmured as his hands slid around Tate's waist and found the warm skin under his polo shirt. "I'm really glad you're here too. Waking up every day with you—that's all I need."

"That, and a good gardener," Tate remarked drily. "I'm pretty sure I saw an orang-utan earlier in that tree." He pointed to a giant tree in the garden laden with some sort of pink bloom. Clay chuckled and kissed the smirk off Tate's face with his usual thoroughness. His hands gripped the back of Tate's head as he pressed his lips against Tate's. Clay's tongue made slow, sensual swirls in his mouth, on his lips, teeth clicking together. Tate had the sense of being emotionally branded and owned and he fucking loved it. Loved that someone like Clay would make him his over and over again.

Clay's hard body pressed against his in a wanton display of possession. His cock pressed against Tate's groin, which was already aflame, and Tate moaned as Clay bit his bottom lip then sucked it into his mouth.

"I need to be inside you," Clay said huskily. "Want to christen the fact you're living here with me by making love to you until you forget who you are. 'Til I forget who I am." He chuckled. "I can feel you're up to it, so maybe we should take this inside?"

Tate finally remembered to breathe. "The study," he gasped as his hands fumbled with Clay's zipper. "I've always had this fantasy about being bent down over that desk and taken and it's the one place we haven't done it yet."

The look in Clay's eyes said he thought that was a great idea. Clay took hold of his arm, propelling him forward as they stumbled to the inner sanctum of Clay's—and now Tate's—home.

Tate's arsehole clenched in anticipation of being bent over that huge leather-topped desk. His dick pushed against the front of his stained and dusty sweats and the minute they reached the room, he tugged off his pants together with his briefs. He breathed a sigh of relief at being free. Pulling his polo shirt over his head, he flung it into the far corner and turned to see Clay pushing his jeans down to his ankles. He made to remove his open-necked button shirt and Tate stopped him.

"Leave the shirt on, just open it." he growled. "I love it when you fuck me that way."

Clay hitched a breath, his green eyes deepening to slits of emerald. "God, you drive me insane when you say things like that." He did as he was told though and his eyes roamed around the room. "I don't think we have lube in here," he muttered. "I think this is the one place—"

He stopped as Tate triumphantly reached under a pile of papers and unearthed a tube.

"You planned this?" Clay's mouth quirked in a grin; a hot, slutty, needy grin that took Tate's breath away.

"Hell yes. I knew we'd need it sometime. Now come here."

Tate drew Clay to him roughly, taking his mouth and groaning as their cocks pressed together, wet and slick, and he knew his was about ready to blow. "God, I want you," he grunted as they rutted together. "There's something about this whole move thing that has made me as randy as fuck."

Clay picked up the lube and opened it, then slid a warm hand down Tate's flank, reaching around to grip the tight globe of his arse. "Bend over," he instructed, his breath deepening as Tate did what he'd been told. He lay flat on the table, arse in the air. He gripped across and over the table, unable to get his hands around the two sides as it was too wide. "I love your arse."

Clay leaned down and kissed Tate's ruined cheek, tracing the dragon scar with his tongue. "I love this." His mouth gently bit at the flesh on his hip. "I love this." His finger slid inside Tate, now coated with cold coffee-scented lube. Tate clenched and unclenched and as another of Clay's fingers pushed inside, he let out a slow growl of satisfaction. He surrendered to the sensation of being filled, and when Clay's cock nudged his hole and slid deep, he gripped the table tighter and pushed back.

They were adept at this slow serenade of lovemaking, of meeting each other's needs and the teasing, needy seduction of skin against skin while mouths grasped greedily at each other's as the chance arose.

Clay's deep sighs as he pushed deep inside Tate were a serenade. Tate made noises of his own when his lover sunk in and touched his prostate, causing his body to spark with fierce, unbridled pleasure. The murmured endearments as Clay made love to Tate made him feel cherished and adored and banished any memories he might have of another time, another place, a tormentor. For Tate, there was only the here and now, as the gentle breeze blew in through an open window and the fragrance of honeysuckle touched his nostrils.

"Going to make you come now," Clay gasped as his hand encircled Tate's cock and he began to stroke it fiercely.

Tate grunted as his swollen prick responded to the movements of Clay's hand. His arse pushed back frantically against Clay as Tate's balls contracted and he covered Clay's hand and desk with warm strings of come that also painted pearly pictures on the floor. The warmth of Clay's own orgasm inside his channel caused Tate to smile fiercely, and he clenched his muscles, milking Clay dry and leaving him a sobbing, gasping mess splayed across Tate's back. Sweat, semen and honeysuckle all combined to make a recipe for a perfume Tate thought he'd definitely buy. It was intoxicating, primal, erotic and all *them*.

Splayed out on the desk like a flattened starfish Tate knew he should have felt uncomfortable but he wasn't. Instead, he twisted so he could embrace that sweaty man of his as he lay heaving above him.

"Hell." Clay's raspy laugh tickled Tate's ear. "There will definitely be more of that. That was fucking hot. *You're* hot." He gripped Tate's face, turning it to face him then seductively licked Tate's mouth. "And you taste like more."

"I'm not sure I can manage that right now," Tate gasped. "But later you can count on me being there."

Tate's skin tingled at Clay's dirty laugh as he slid out of him and moved away.

Tate groaned as he unglued himself from the desk. "I got spunk everywhere," he moaned as he stood up and stretched. "Do we have a housekeeper?"

Clay snorted. "No housekeeper. Just good old wet wipes and Kleenex." He rummaged in a small wooden cabinet and Tate raised an eyebrow when he produced said goods.

"You've done this sort of thing before then, to have *that* in there?" Tate gestured to the items Clay was using to clean up, feeling a prickle of jealousy that perhaps maybe he hadn't been the first one to be had on Clay's table that way. He tore a piece of tissue off and wiped up the random spooge that glistened on the side of the desk.

"No," Clay said softly. "I've never fucked anyone in here. Only you. It's just I have a habit of coffee spills and ink stains. And you don't want to see what my hands look like when I change the printer cartridges."

"Oh." Tate felt better at that. "Not that it matters, of course." He gave a careless shrug. "I mean you had a life before me."

Clay reached over and caressed Tate's cheek, his green eyes warm with satisfaction at the jealousy in Tate's tone. "Liar," he said softly. "I *had* no life before I had you in it like this."

Tate's throat closed at that statement and he was horrified to feel a prickle of tears behind his eyes. He coughed to cover it up.

Since when did I become so damn needy?

"Sex makes you all emotional," he murmured. "You want to watch that. It could be catching."

He didn't miss Clay's smile as he finished cleaning up and tossed the dirty wipes and tissue into the waste bin. His boyfriend looked decadent standing there in only an open shirt, his cock hanging heavy between his legs and trails of dried come on his stomach.

Tate looked down at himself and grinned when he realised he looked even more debauched. He was naked, with dried come everywhere. His arsehole hurt too. "Maybe we should get in the shower and clean this off. I think I need a little TLC; my backside feels as if it's had a tree trunk rammed in it."

He sauntered out of the door into the hallway, and along to the winding stairs. The best shower in the house was upstairs in the master bedroom. Tate had a hankering to see what it felt like being in there as master of the house and not an overnighter. Judging from the footsteps following him up the stairs, and the hand resting lightly on his back, Tate had a feeling he wouldn't be in there alone.

Chapter 15

Liquorice had never been one of Clay's favourite things to eat. Even more so when it was covered with lint and speckles of dust. He and Tate had the same dislike of the stuff.

His boyfriend had left him in the small reception room at Castaways while he went to find the famous, or infamous, Jax that Tate talked about incessantly. He had promised to take Jax to Tate's usual hangout to do some graffiti painting. He'd wanted Clay to come along to meet his new young 'apprentice.'

Clay prayed that Tate going back to where Lily had died wouldn't affect him and push him back to that dark place he'd lived in for so long. Christ, he was moving forward now and Clay didn't want that to change. Tate hadn't been back to the abandoned baths since Lily's suicide. While he had quietly assured his lover he was fine with it, Clay had to decide whether to trust Tate's judgment or hover, which, Clay admitted, hadn't gone down well in the past. He worried over it, but at the end of the day, he wasn't going to undo all the progress they had made by letting his insecurities for Tate's well-being colour the outing.

The problem now? Clay hadn't been left alone. He'd been quickly introduced and now two small faces watched him eagerly as their proffered gift of a string of apple-scented green liquorice had been pressed into his hand. Before he'd sped up the stairs, Tate had chuckled and said he thought it was some baptism of fire all newbies went through. Clay hadn't quite understood it at the time.

The two children, introduced as Damien and Krispin, stared at him expectantly. They didn't seem to say much at all. There had been some shy smiles, some giggling and a few whispers between them and that had been it.

Clay cleared his throat. He was obviously expected to eat the item he'd been given. Or perhaps he could be the bigger person and say he was saving it for Tate. That thought made him hopeful. He was about to declare his noble intention when someone tweaked the skin on his ribs and he uttered a soft curse as he turned to face his pincher.

Tate stood there, a young, blond man beside him, and Clay was stunned. When'd he expected to see Jackson Grady, he hadn't expected to meet a flawed angel. The man was simply breathtakingly beautiful, even with the scars on his face and the blue eyes that regarded him evenly from underneath a tilted chin.

"Aren't you going to eat that?" Tate gestured to the item in his hand with a smirk.

Clay stared at the liquorice. "I, er, I thought I'd save it for you," he muttered, knowing Tate would see through that but giving it a shot anyway.

Tate shook his head vehemently. "Oh no, I insist you have it. I've already had a bit."

Jax chuckled softly and placed a hand on Tate's arm. Clay narrowed his eyes, knowing it was childish to be jealous of a seventeen-year-old.

"It's a thing with Damien," Jax said, his voice deep and rich. "Think of it like a university hazing ritual."

Clay glanced at the kids watching him and decided *fuck it.* He'd been in the SAS, and a sweet and two kids weren't going to get the better of him. He popped the green string in his mouth and chewed it. It was really sour and his eyes began to water.

"Fuck," he sucked his lips together as the sourness intensified. Tate laughed loudly and placed big hands over the little kids' ears.

Clay's face burned with guilt. "Sorry about the swearword, but, wow. That's a little tart." He managed to swallow it at last.

The two children were giggling and smirking, no doubt at Clay's language. Jax grinned and went over to the boys. He leaned down and whispered something in their ear and their faces lit up.

"Really?" Damien's face lit up and Krispin seemed to look at Clay with a new respect. "Will he do it for us?"

"Maybe one day," Jax promised and Clay wondered what the hell he was in for now. "But right now, you guys need to disappear into the garden and go find Jen. She has a picnic outside for you."

With whoops of glee, the two boys ran out of the room.

Clay narrowed his eyes in suspicion at an innocent-looking Jax. Tate was grinning from ear to ear and Clay wondered what they'd been cooking up.

"What have you promised I'd show them?"

"Don't blame Jax. It was my idea." Tate grinned. "The kids have an outing coming up and they all wanted to go the airfield to see the planes take off and have a barbeque. I might have suggested to young Jax here that you could parachute out of a plane while we were there."

Clay's jaw dropped. "Honestly?" He could do that with his eyes closed but he wasn't sure he wanted to be a fair-side attraction.

Tate snorted. "Yes, Mister SAS man. It would mean a lot to the kids to see someone they knew doing that. And you have to keep up your jumping hours so I thought it might make a nice trip out for us. I mean we're talking you, jumping out of a plane." He grinned wolfishly. "That's something I'd like to see myself. Hell, maybe I'd join you."

Clay didn't miss the look of yearning that crossed Jax's face at Tate's words.

"You ever thought of doing something like that, Jax?" Clay asked softly.

Jax started, nibbling on his lips. "I'd love to do that. Jump out of a plane. Feel the wind racing through my hair, the rush…" His voice tailed off.

Tate reached over and chucked Jax on the chin with a mock fist. "I'm sure we could organise a tandem jump…?" His eyes searched Clay's.

Clay nodded. "Of course, that shouldn't be a problem. Jax could jump with me when we do this whole day out."

He warmed at seeing the expression of gratitude in Tate's eyes. His man really had a bond with the young man.

Jax's face brightened. "I could do that? I'd need to check with the doctors though that they don't have any objections. My eyes might need some special covering or something so they don't get damaged, but hell, I'd love to do it if I can."

"Then it's settled." Tate gave Clay a quick smile. "I'll talk to Randy and he can find out what we need to do to get this medically approved. The last thing we want is anything happening to what's left of your sight."

Jax gave a wide beam and Clay's heart melted. Between Jax and Leslie Scott, Clay's whole tough-guy act was going out the window. He'd have loved to have had a child; a son would have been nice. He sighed. It wasn't really something they talked about too seriously other than in passing, but he knew Tate had been averse to the idea before. Now? Perhaps. He wanted to pursue the marriage idea with Tate once again; talk to him about it and see how he felt because, really, who knew? Anything was possible in this ever-changing relationship they had; even the prospect of having a child one day.

Clay was interrupted from his musings by Tate's heavy thump to his arm. "Hey," he glared at his boyfriend. "What the hell?"

Tate mock boxed around him, throwing fake punches. "You looked in a brown study there. We need to get going. I've got an art lesson to give to my protégé here…"

He picked up his rucksack, which Clay knew was loaded with paint tins, and slung it across his shoulder. Tate helped Jax get his own satchel on board then turned to Clay with a raised eyebrow.

"Right, we're ready. Let's go. We've got trains to catch and it's a bit of a trip. I need coffee; we need to stop at Starbucks. And maybe a Danish or something. I'm starving."

Clay rolled his eyes and laughed when he saw Jax doing the same thing. This was going to be an interesting afternoon.

****

When they got to the derelict swimming bath with its concrete canvases, Tate got quieter as they walked toward a wall emblazoned with a green-clad clockwork man. Clay recognised Tate's tag on the side of the mural.

"You okay, baby?" Clay murmured softly. He'd noticed Tate's stillness and the stiffer body language as they approached the wall.

Tate nodded. "Yeah." He grinned softly. "I'm the big, tough cop, remember?"

Clay reached out and squeezed his hand. "I remember."

Tate smiled softly. "Besides, this isn't for me. It's for Jax. He needs a boost. I think he'll get a kick out of it."

Clay chuckled. "I never thought I'd see the day my 'big, tough cop' got all soft over a teenager." He reached up and brushed Tate's cheek softly. "I'm so damn proud of you. You've been great with him and he really likes you. Trusts you. It's a big thing inspiring someone like that."

Tate looked over at Jax. "He's a great kid. It's like having a kid brother. I like it."

Jax gave them a both a faint smile as he walked beside them.

On the train, the teenager had been quiet, gazing down at the floor of the tube behind dark sunglasses and gripping his satchel tightly. Tate had spoken quietly to him and Jax had nodded and then stuck his earbuds in his ears and listened to music on his mobile phone. On the walk to the complex, Jax had insisted he could walk on his own.

Tate and Clay had made sure to be either side of him, as he walked *über* carefully, chin held high. When he'd stumbled once or twice, misjudging a step or the kerb, both of them had swiftly steadied him. Clay wasn't sure how much was politically correct and what could be construed as patronising. He was following Tate's lead, as he seemed to have Jax's measure.

As they drew closer to the wall, Clay nudged Tate and gestured to the picture. "I like it. Very expressive. Feeling a bit manipulated at the time, were you?" He knew Tate's murals depicted his moods and he was pretty adept at picking up on his lover's emotions.

Tate stared at the man with faraway eyes. "Yeah. Something like that."

Beside him, Jax murmured softly.

Clay wasn't sure what he'd said, and whether it had been at his words or the picture itself. He stood, unsure what to do next. So he sat down against the wall, crossed his legs in front of him and leant back. Then he waited for his two damaged souls to take the lead. He closed his eyes, enjoying the afternoon sunshine. In the far corner of the quadrant, older youths swore and joshed with each other and he heard the rattling of paint cans.

"So what are we doing then?" asked Jax uncertainly. "I haven't painted anything in a while. I'm not sure I remember how to."

Clay opened his eyes to see Tate's empathic glance at his young friend.

"You paint from the heart, Jax," Tate murmured softly, pressing a primed paint can into Jax's hand. "You aim the nozzle and in your mind, you see what you want to say. I've seen your paintings. You're good and your instincts will take over. Pick a spot and just let yourself go." He reached out and ruffled Jax's blond curls affectionately. "Do anything you want."

Jax nodded and shuffled over to a blank bit of wall. He considered it for a while, in a birdlike fashion with his delicate chin raised. Clay saw the fingers of his free hand clenching and unclenching. Then he lifted his paint can and began spraying.

Clay didn't have a creative painting bone in his body. He could write a bit and had published a few articles on violence, life in the military and such for various publications. But drawing anything meaningful other than a stick figure—*that* he couldn't do. He admired people who could translate their emotions into painting and/or graffiti like this.

He watched Tate as he studied the wall, rubbing his chin, raising his arms and sketching something in the air. Tate nodded once or twice, deep in thought, then aimed his spray tin and painted a white swatch on the wall. The rebel that dwelt inside him was taking over, flaunting convention and leaving his lasting mark.

Clay loved seeing him like that—immersed in his task, so focused on what he was doing that everything else disappeared. Including Clay, he realised ruefully.

He closed his eyes and enjoyed the warmth of the sun, its soft touch making him drowsy. Around him, he heard the hiss of cans, the murmurings as Tate or Jax pondered their mural, soft huffs from Tate as he worked and in the distance, faint shouts and laughter from no doubt other graffiti artists, who were busy making their mark. It was peaceful, and the sun was warm and Clay relaxed.

"Wow. He looks so peaceful, seems a shame to wake him up." Jax's voice with its hint of laughter roused Clay and he opened his eyes to see Tate and Jax peering down at him. He swallowed; his throat dry, his eyes slightly gritty. He hoped like hell he hadn't been drooling.

I must have fallen asleep.

His boyfriend observed him with a sly glint in his eye. "Afternoon, old-timer. You were having a nice snooze but it's getting late so we thought we'd better wake you up."

Clay scowled. "Fuck off. Enough of the 'old,' thanks."

He squinted up at the two men sniggering above him. "Are you two done creating the new Picassos?"

He clambered to his feet and looked over at the walls, which had once been plain and grey and now abounded with colour. The pictures leapt off the wall and assaulted his eyes with a visual feast that was both bold and vibrant. They took his breath away. His Picasso comment hadn't been far off the mark.

"What do you think?" Tate asked, and Clay heard the hesitation in his voice.

He shook his head in wonder. "Baby, it looks—wow. Just damn wow. And Jax—I hope I'm not being PC here, but hell, you paint better with bad sight than I could ever hope to manage fully sighted and with a modicum of talent. It's stunning, truly."

Jax's face flushed in pleasure and he shifted on his feet. "Thanks," he said awkwardly. "I just did like Tate told me to. Let my instinct guide me. And Tate's mural is radical. He is really talented." He threw Tate a look of hero worship and Clay bit back a smile. That look on Jax's face was the way he felt every minute of the day.

Tate's mural was about five feet high, the same wide and was rainbow coloured; a giant pink dragon graced the wall, orange fire blowing from its nostrils. In the belly of the dragon, the initials AK were written in bright, vivid green. The dragon held a small green and white flower in its outstretched claws. Tate's signature tag of his initials formed the prong of the dragon's tail. Clay's heart ached at what his rebellious lover had done and he had to push down the emotion that swelled inside.

"It's a mural for Lily," he said softly, looking at Tate, who was observing his creation with critical eyes. "You said she wanted a pink dragon and you gave her one."

Tate nodded. "I wanted her to know she hadn't been forgotten, that she was real, hence the AK. It was who she was, even if she called herself Lily when I met her." He scowled. "I'm not good with flowers, so hopefully that looks like a lily. Maybe I should try and get it a little more defined—"

Jax reached over and gripped Tate's arm. "It looks perfect to me," he said gently. "Leave it. If it's a little flawed in your eyes, that just makes it all the more real."

Tate frowned at his protégé. "Since when you did you get so damn smart? That sounds like something Clay would have said." But he smiled, his face softening. "Love, what do you think of Jax's music score? Isn't it sheer genius?" He beamed with pride and Clay's heart once again swelled with emotion.

God, this man will be the death of me. How did I get so damn lucky to have a man like Tate?

"It's phenomenal," he agreed, looking at the three-foot mural of a music sheet with notes, clefs, staffs and various other symbols imprinted upon it. It was classic black and white, and had a white space in the middle in which a figure, roughly drawn in black, sat gazing up around him at the detail of the sheet. It lacked the detail of Tate's creations, and there were places where paint had run and overlapped. But it was beautifully expressed and instantly recognisable. For a young man who was half blind and hadn't touched paint in years, it was an incredible feat of perseverance. Something Clay understood all too well in his struggle to rescue Tate from his demons.

"I'm speechless, actually, Jax. Is that you in the middle? Is music something you enjoy?"

Jax nodded, and a shy smile crossed his face. "I love music. I was taking piano lessons when I got hurt and I had to give it up." His face shadowed. "I wanted to do it again but I just couldn't. I kept thinking it would be too damn hard and I couldn't see the sheet music or the keys and it would just be too damn awkward, plus who's got patience to teach a half-blind guy the piano?" The words rushed out like a verbal assault. "I enjoyed the music side more than the painting. I even wrote some songs."

Clay reached him before Tate did and laid a finger on Jax's lips. "Stevie Wonder plays the piano and he's been completely blind from birth. You can do it, Jax. You're a remarkable young man. You'll find a way to bring the music back. I have no doubt. And if we can help at all, you let us know."

Tate nodded and reached out and pummelled Jax on the arm. "What he said. He's pretty wise for an old, sleepy geezer." He threw a blinding smile at Clay and then bent down to start shoving empty paint cans into his bag. "Come on. We need to get this cleaned up—"

Just then, two youths that had been loitering on the periphery sidled up to them. Clay tensed but Tate nodded at them.

"Freddy. Mitch. How's it hanging, guys?"

The tall, skinny, ebony-skinned teen of about sixteen bobbed his head and reached out to fist pump Tate's outstretched knuckles. The other teen, a pale kid around the same age with untidy ginger hair, stood shuffling next to him.

"Coo, dude, cool. Me and my homey Mitch here are liking that dragon. The music one's not bad either." The boys' eyes flittered to Clay and he tried not to look threatening as he smiled at them.

Jax stood quietly, hands clutching his satchel. His chin lifted as he watched the other two young men.

"So." Freddy nodded then turned to look at Tate. "Is that for Lily? You're the guy who found her, right?" His jaw tightened.

Tate nodded. "Yeah. It's for Lily. She deserved it."

Freddy's head bobbed up and down fiercely. "That she did, man. She was legend. Such a damn little trooper. Me and Mitch here, we tried to get her to hospital to see about that cough, but she was having none of it. Bit our heads off if we even mentioned it." His face darkened. "Damn shame she did what she did. Sorry you had to find her that way, bro. Musta been a shock."

"Yeah." Tate's Adam's apple bobbed as he swallowed. "But it's done. And now she has a dragon to watch over her, so," he shrugged. "It is what it is."

"Word," Mitch finally said solemnly, darting a curious glance at Jax. "You did some damn fine art there, with the music shit. Looks good."

"Thanks," Jax murmured. "It's my first time."

Mitch stared at him. "Cool." He stood staring at Jax, and Clay saw the teen's face begin to flush.

Mitch gave Jax a huge grin. "You're really fucking beautiful, you know that?"

Jax's face went bright pink and he fumbled with the straps of his rucksack. Clay was pretty sure that speechless was a rare occasion for him. He swallowed a snort of laughter and Tate seemed to be doing the same.

"Er, thanks," Jax stammered.

Freddy smacked his friend on the back of his head, causing Mitch to yowl in pain. "You got no manners, you know that? Don't go telling guys that sort of thing unless you really know they swing your way, you fucking idiot. How many times do I have to tell ya?"

He cast an apologetic glance at them all. "Please don't beat us up, I'm really fucking sorry. Mitch here is a *homosekshual*," he drawled the word teasingly, "and his mouth runs away with him sometimes."

Clay wanted to burst into laughter. It sounded like the two things weren't mutually exclusive and it amused him no end.

"No problem," he said, seeing the glisten of tears in Tate's eyes as he tried to hold back his own mirth. "No offence taken." He glanced at Jax, whose face was less red now and whose lips curved in a slight smile.

"Well, we need to get off." Freddy announced with a dark glare at his friend, "Before my friend here decides to hump yours and then we'll really be in trouble. Later, dudes."

He yanked Mitch's arm and the two men walked away, Mitch casting a cheeky grin over his shoulder at Jax, whose smile grew wider. Clay was still struggling to hold back breaking into great guffaws of pure amusement.

Tate reached out and bumped Jax's shoulder with his. "See? I told you people would find you cute," he teased. "Mitch thinks you're beautiful, Jax. It's those blond curls."

"Fuck off," Jax said with a smirk. Tate chuckled and finished picking up the cans and stuffing them in his bag. Clay knew Jax hadn't definitely come out and said he was gay to Tate, but it was something Tate suspected. Based on his reaction today, Clay thought it was probably the case. Jax hadn't appeared uncomfortable at all with Mitch's admiration; he had in fact welcomed it.

Clay watched as Tate bent down and his arse strained the seams of the tight black jeans he wore, jeans that were stained with pink paint. Clay decided that later he'd definitely be peeling them off his lover and perhaps even putting the study desk to good use again. He stood back and took one last look at the murals that had sprung from nothing into statements of affection, remembrance and compassion. Tate looked at Clay and the love in his eyes spoke volumes. Clay grinned back at him and hoped his eyes conveyed the same look.

Oh yes, there was definitely going to be crazy, passionate sex when they got home. Then pizza. With anchovies, whether Tate liked it or not. Clay thought that might be the perfect ending to a perfect day.

Chapter 16

Seven p.m. on a Friday night and Tate was on his way back from a retirement party being held for a fellow policeman. The local pub near the police station where he'd worked was warm, friendly and had cheap drinks. Tate was driving so he hadn't imbibed too much. On a whim, knowing Clay was working late tonight (having texted him only ten minutes before) he decided to pay his boyfriend a late-night visit at the office.

Maybe we can catch a quick drink together before going home.

Happy with his plan, Tate swiped his own office key card to gain access to the building and took the lift up to Clay's office. He knocked briefly on the door and entered. He didn't bother waiting to be allowed in.

As he stepped inside Clay's office, his partner waved a hand at him, motioning to him to sit down. The scowl Clay had on his face disappeared momentarily at the sight of Tate to be replaced by a warm, albeit distracted grin. The scowl was soon back in all its ferocity. His mobile was glued to his ear and Tate bit back a grin at the poor unfortunate soul on the other side of the phone who was earning Clay's ire. Tate made himself comfortable in the plush visitor's chair in front of Clay's desk and sat back to enjoy the show.

He admired the sight of his man standing in full aggression mode. Tate drank in the sexy lines of Clay's broad shoulders in his rumpled white shirt, top button open, tie loosely slung around his neck. The tight curve of Clay's arse in his dark blue trousers and the shirtsleeves rolled up to his elbows was another tantalising image. Tate's cock began to swell, his fantasies taking reign. In his mind, he slowly undressed Clay, unzipping his trousers, pushing them down around his ankles and then slowly, teasingly, undoing the buttons on his shirt one by one…

"Fuck you, you miserable piece of shit." Clay's infuriated roar jolted Tate out of his dirty daydream. He sat up upright, watching Clay as he stormed around the room, phone gripped tightly in clenched fingers. "Don't you fucking tell me I can't fucking get my guy out of that damn place. Find me a way to get Graham out of that fucking hellhole. I don't care what it costs. The man has family waiting for him back here, and the last thing I want is him rotting in an Estonian prison cell. You're the negotiator. Fucking negotiate!"

There was a loud quacking sound from the other side of the phone and Tate raised an eyebrow as Clay looked over at him and shrugged apologetically.

Tate shook his head and gave Clay a slow smile. "Don't stop on my account," he murmured softly. "I think it's hot, you getting so mad. All that testosterone makes me horny." He ran a hand suggestively over the front of his jeans where the outline of his hard-on was already evident. Clay's face flushed and his eyes darkened. Tate licked his lips and chuckled when Clay turned away from him, obviously intent on ignoring his seduction. He continued his conversation with the negotiator on the phone.

"That sounds like a better idea; now you're talking my language. Like I said, no problem with expenses. Just get the man back home. Phone me later. Let me know when I can tell Janey she'll have her husband back. And Wally, don't fucking let me down. Or I will come over there, hunt you down and kill you myself."

The threat in his voice was unmistakeable. Tate was now so turned on it was all he could do not to bend Clay over his desk, rip his trousers off and take him right there. He gave a satisfied chuckle at that thought and tried to look innocent as Clay slammed his phone down on his desk and glared at him.

"What?" Tate said indignantly. "I'm not allowed to have fantasies?"

"Fantasies?" Clay growled. "You looked like you were about to blow right there. You had that look on your face."

Tate stood up and sauntered over to Clay, who leaned back against the desk, arms folded across his chest. His green eyes were watchful, but there was the hint of a grin on his lips. From the looks of the bulge in his crotch, he was beginning to get turned on too.

"What look?" Tate asked as he reached out a hand and slid Clay's tie through his fingers. "The one that says I find you so damn sexy I can't keep my hands off you?" He twirled the tie around in his fingers. "The one that says I want to rip your clothes off and fuck you right now?"

Clay's breathing was shallow, his pupils dark as he watched Tate's mouth. Tate was having a bit of trouble of breathing too. "Or the one that says that I want to taste you in my mouth, right here, right now?" He leaned in and swiped his tongue over Clay's lips, loving Clay's throaty moan. He pushed against Clay, rubbing their groins together as Clay gripped the side of his desk, knuckles white.

"We can't do this in here," he groaned softly. Tate brushed his hand against Clay's cock, which pushed forward instinctively. "There are cameras everywhere."

"I like the idea of putting on a show," Tate whispered in Clay's ear, as his tongue delved into its depths. A delicious shiver ran through Clay's body. Tate loved it. Loved that he could do this to a man who with one phone call could probably start a small war in some distant country. He loved hearing Clay's breaths deepen and his eyes become black as his pupils dilated with pleasure. He loved the control he currently had over this man who meant the world to him.

"We can't…" Clay groaned again. "I'm the damn boss, the last thing I need is them seeing me with my arse in the air with you inside me."

Tate's dick grew harder. "You want me to take you?" He licked a trail from Clay's jaw up to his mouth. Clay's lips parted and Tate slid his tongue against Clay's eager one then pulled away. "Push inside you until you scream, ram my hard prick into you and call your name when I come?"

Clay's breathing was ragged. His hands had slid inside Tate's shirt, finding warm skin, and Tate was in need of more of Clay's naked skin himself. "Christ, Tate. We need to go somewhere else to finish this, baby. It's gone too far already." He pulled away from Tate, slipping to the side and zipping himself up. He took Tate's hand and motioned to the door. "Come with me. I know where we can continue this seduction you have going."

Tate gave a sultry laugh as he was dragged out of Clay's office. "Seduction? Is that what I'm doing?"

Clay nodded as he tugged Tate along the darkened corridor. "Oh yes. That's exactly what you have going. And may I say I like it, so don't stop." He halted at a closed door and looked back at Tate, his eyes quirking devilishly. "This room has no cameras. You've been here so you know it's pretty comfy. Come on." He opened the door and pulled Tate inside.

The office common room, known fondly as the Chill Room by the employees, had a couple of couches, a luxurious shaggy pile rug and even a fireplace. In winter, the fireplace burned cosily and the room became a haven to escape the pressures and often ugly aspects of the work Clay's team did. As they entered the room, Tate found himself propelled backward to the floor, landing on the thick rug with an 'oomph' as Clay towered above him, fingers already unzipping his jeans.

"Oh no, you don't," Tate muttered and with one limber move, he shot up, unseated Clay from his hips and had him pinned beneath him. Clay shouted out in surprise but didn't struggle. Instead, he relaxed and grinned as he lay back, stretching his arms above his head with an air of nonchalance.

"I see which way this is going," he said, lips curving into a soft smile. "I hope you brought lube with you because I sure as hell don't have any in here."

Tate smirked. "I do, actually." Tate reached around to his back pocket and drew out his wallet. "It's only a sachet but I think it'll do."

"You *think*?" Clay's eyes widened in apprehension. "Hell, you'd better make sure it's mega-size for that huge cock of yours to fit in me. Economy just won't do."

Tate chuckled again and drew out the sachet. "I'll get you ready," he said slyly. Tate straddled Clay and once again unzipped him. "Up," he commanded and Clay obeyed, lifting his hips so Tate could draw the trousers and his boxers off his lean hips. "Turn over," he instructed, kneeling over Clay.

Clay did as he was told and was soon face-down on the rug, on his knees with legs apart. Tate could have spent hours staring at that sexy sight—Clay clad only in his shirt and tie, his tight, rounded backside, the dusky puckered hole, the balls that hung low with the jutting cock as Clay moaned and rutted down against the rug.

"Christ, hurry up and do something will you? I need you."

Tate stroked Clay's cheeks and ran his hands loving down his lover's hips. "Patience, you randy bastard. Who's running this show?"

"You," Clay whispered as his hips thrust against the rug. "Always you."

Those husky words spurred Tate, their timbre and passion inciting the flame in his groin and in his heart. He stood up and dropped his jeans and briefs to the floor, leaving his shirt on. Then he knelt down behind the prone and groaning man on the floor and ripped open the lube. Tate's own dick was so hard he thought he might have been able to drive nails into the wall with it. He was already leaking and wet and ready to be buried inside Clay. He dripped the lube onto Clay's hole, hearing Clay's hiss of pleasure, then slowly, deliberately, he pulled Clay's cheeks apart, thumbs sliding inside his man, widening him, delving deeper and deeper as Clay moaned in ecstasy.

"Oh, God, Tate, your fingers. It feels so good, love. Want your cock inside me, need to feel you. Love to feel you split me open, own me. Please, make love to me. Now."

Seeing Clay come apart in this way thrilled Tate in a way nothing else could. His tough man, his protector...the tables were turned and now it was Tate's turn to make sure Clay got what he needed.

"I'll make love to you," he whispered as he pushed inside that warm, tight place. "Not fucking tonight. Want to make you feel good."

Clay's groans below him as he rocked back against Tate's cock, impaling himself deeper, turned Tate's insides to mush. Clay's moans and whispered entreaties to go deeper was what Tate needed. He loved to see Clay give up, be taken and controlled. He wanted to be the one giving solace to him, loving him.

As they moved together as one, slow strokes and muffled cries, the fusion of their bodies performed a dance of both adoration and possession of each other, and to Tate, the world seemed to stop. His dick was aching for release and as he moved toward the welcome sensation of spilling his seed inside the man he loved, he whispered Clay's name.

That single utterance pushed Clay toward his orgasm. Clay shuddered beneath Tate as he came, muscles tightening around Tate's cock, causing him to lose him breath. As Clay emptied himself onto the rug, Tate cried out softly and gave one last thrust, then pulsed inside his lover, filling him and spending everything he had in payment of his debt of love. Boneless and content, Tate kissed Clay's shoulder, dropped soft kisses across his back, before moving out and off him to lie beside on the rug. The air had grown chilled and both of them shivered as they lay there half naked.

"I'm cold but I can't get up," Clay murmured as he raised a hand to stroke Tate's cheek tenderly.

Tate closed his eyes at that gesture. "Uh-huh. Me too." He snorted. "This rug of yours is going to need cleaning. There's spunk everywhere."

Clay waved a hand tiredly. "I'm sure it's seen worse. I'm not too sure what goes on in here after hours. I'll get it cleaned up."

He leaned up on one elbow and gazed down into Tate's eyes. "Thank you," he whispered softly and traced Tate's lips with a finger.

"For what?"

"For being here. For making love to me like you did tonight. For moving in with me. For just being you. Tate Williams. The man I love."

Tate's throat closed up with emotion at those heartfelt words. "I love you too, Clay Mortimer. I doubt I'd be here if it wasn't for you. I know I'm a pain in the arse sometimes, but you keep forgiving me, taking me back."

Clay chuckled. "Pain in the arse is right. There could have been a tad more lube." His face softened. "And forgiving is all part of loving someone." He shivered. "I don't want to break up the romance but I'm fucking freezing. What say we get dressed and get home, get into bed and we can do a little more lovemaking? Where it's nice and warm." He shivered again, goose bumps breaking out on his skin.

Tate nodded and struggled to his feet. "I say a big fat yes to that proposal." He hunted around for his pants and put them on, watching Clay do the same. "Can we go home in your car, and I'll pick mine up tomorrow? I don't think I've enough energy to drive."

Clay rolled his eyes. "I guess. I'll need to pick up my keys from my office. Let me go get them." He gave Tate a lingering kiss from cold lips then disappeared into the hallway. Tate followed, limbs tired, body satisfied and heart warmed.

When he got to Clay's office, Tate saw him standing there, holding a small white card in his hand. Clay turned, almost guiltily, as he came in. He seemed a little uncertain of himself,

"What you got there? Are you ordering Chinese? Is it from Wongs or that other place?" Tate reached out to take the card and Clay held it away.

"No, it's not bloody Chinese. It's something I was going to give you tomorrow, but I think maybe I should give it to you now." Clay shrugged. "I think the time is right."

Tate's curiosity was piqued. "What is it?"

Clay handed him the card silently and cocked his head to one side, waiting.

Tate stared down at the card and his eyes prickled uncomfortably. He looked down at the card, then up at Clay. "Is this for real?"

The business card read:

Tate Williams. Lead Investigator, Mortimer Investigations.

Clay nodded. "Of course it is. You deserve to come on board more than anyone I know. It's time you went back out into the field. You're ready and I want you to know I have faith in you." He shuffled uncomfortably. "I also want to talk to you about becoming a partner in the business, a shareholder, with equal rights. I want us to manage this business together. But I guess that's a conversation for—oomph."

He didn't finish his sentence because Tate's mouth was on his, kissing him with every fibre of his being. Tate wrapped his arms around Clay's neck and held on as passion and love spent itself in every flick of a tongue, every press of lips against lips and every soft murmur of breath into each other's mouths.

Finally Tate let Clay go and rested his forehead against his lover's. "Thanks," he said huskily. "For believing in me."

"That's no hardship, love," Clay said softly as he nudged Tate's nose with his. "It's a privilege."

He grinned and moved to pick up his keys from his desk.

Tate's heart was full and he had no more words. They'd both come a long way since those early days of pain and grief. It had taken endurance and patience on both their sides to get to where they were now. It had taken a feat of Clay.

Tate knew he would still have some way to go to be completely healed and that perhaps he might never put his ordeal totally behind him. But he had Clay. And friends. People who cared about him. Some people didn't have the half of what he had.

Clay was his rock, his soul mate. And Tate knew without a shadow of doubt that he was Clay's. And that simple fact meant that whatever life might throw at them in the future, whatever dangers or sadness they may encounter, they would do it together.

ABOUT THE AUTHOR

Susan Mac Nicol is a self-confessed bookaholic, an avid watcher of videos of sexy pole-dancing men, a self-confessed geek and nerd, and in love with her Smartphone. This little treasure is called 'the boyfriend' by her longsuffering husband, who says if it vibrated there'd be no need for him. Susan hasn't had the heart to tell him there's an app for that.

A lover of walks in the forest, theatre productions, dabbling her toes in the cold North Sea and the vibrant city of London where you can experience all four seasons in a day, she is a hater of pantomime (please don't tar and feather her), duplicitous people, bigotry and self-righteous idiots. She likes to think of herself as a 'half full' kind of gal, although sometimes that philosophy is sorely tested.

In an ideal world, Susan Mac Nicol would be Queen of England and banish all the bad people to the Never Never Lands of Wherever-Who Cares. As that's not going to happen, she contents herself with writing her HEA stories and pretending that, just for a little while, good things happen to good people.

OTHER BOOKS BY SUSAN MAC NICOL

Stripped Bare
Saving Alexander
Worth Keeping
Double Alchemy
Double Alchemy:
Climax
Love and Punishment

THE MEN OF LONDON SERIES

Love You Senseless
Sight & Sinners
Suit Yourself

THE STARLIGHT SERIES

Cassandra by Starlight
Together in Starlight

Did you enjoy this book? Drop us a line and say so! We love to hear from readers, and so do our authors. To connect, visit www.boroughspublishinggroup.com online, send comments directly to info@boroughspublishinggroup.com, or friend us on Facebook and Twitter. And be sure to check back regularly for contests and new releases in your favorite subgenres of romance!

Are you an aspiring writer? Check out www.boroughspublishinggroup.com/submit and see if we can help you make your dreams come true.

www.ingramcontent.com/pod-product-compliance
Lightning Source LLC
Chambersburg PA
CBHW070930130626
46555CB00001B/365